Go Go Dancer

C. C. Varnell

Go-Go Dancer: A Tale of Love and Illusion in Paradise, Phuket Thailand *by C.C. Varnell*

Copyright © 2025 by C.C. Varnell All rights reserved.

Cover design © 2025 by C.C. Varnell

Published by Kindle Direct Publishing

ISBN: 979-8-9930400-1-1

First Edition August 1, 2025

For permissions requests, contact:ccvarnellbooks@gmail.com

Printed in the United States of America (for paperback editions)

Contents

Introduction

"Love is a battlefield." – **Pat Benatar**

SOME PEOPLE WILL TELL you love is simple—two people meet, sparks ignite, and destiny unfolds like clockwork. Others will argue that love is complicated, messy, a tangle of emotions and miscalculations that lead inevitably to heartbreak. Both perspectives are incomplete; love, at its core, is neither easy nor complex—it is strategic warfare, a power struggle cloaked in seduction, desire, and illusion.

So perhaps you picked up this book expecting a leisurely travel romance, a voyeuristic escape into the sensual and mysterious depths of a kingdom renowned for its smiles, yet infamous for its shadows. Perhaps you anticipate intrigue, the thrill of forbidden romance, the lush chaos that pulses through the neon-lit heart of Thailand. Or perhaps you sense already that this might be your own story, reflected back to you through the looking glass of another's mistakes. All these expectations are valid, and all will be rewarded—but none of them quite capture the full truth.

As you prepare to embark on this journey, heed one caution: resist the temptation to skip ahead, to decipher the outcome too swiftly, for it is not in the resolution but in the unfolding of each calculated maneuver, each carefully executed seduction, each intimate deception, that the true richness of this story lies.

Thailand does not simply enter your life. It invades it like a dream you can't shake, an addiction you can't break. You don't merely visit Thailand—you orbit it, compelled by forces stronger than reason, more powerful than caution. It begins innocently enough with fantasy: the careful planning, the slow-building anticipation that teases your imagination long before your feet touch the humid ground. Then comes the journey itself—seductive, dangerous, dizzyingly alive—and the consequences that inevitably follow.

The crash is hardest when you return home, where familiar comforts suddenly feel bland, ordinary life pale and muted. Your memories take on a seductive glow, vivid and irresistible. Thailand whispers from afar, promising that the next time will be different, better, and that the illusion can become reality. And like the addict you've unknowingly become, you believe it again and again. But transformation never comes cheaply, and Thailand exacts a price few anticipate and even fewer escape paying.

This is one of those stories—about a transformation bought at the highest emotional cost. It's about a man, who we will name "Chase", who sought adventure, seduced by illusions of control and conquest, believing that he was the master strategist, immune to emotional weakness or the wiles of women of the night. But it is about a woman, who we will name "Fern", who craved intimacy yet idealized detachment, fiercely guarding her independence, convinced she was the one always in command. Both perhaps too clever for their own good, but also perhaps not really that smart at all, only you reader can be the judge of that.

They thought they were different, immune, special—masters of deception and seduction, adept at the art of controlled vulnerability. Each believed the other was the conquest, a mere opponent in the grand game of emotional warfare. What they didn't foresee was how deeply they would come to need the lie, how truth, vulnerability, and genuine connection would emerge as threats greater than any enemy they could anticipate.

The most dangerous games are never played on a field, table, or a game board, but rather are played in the heart. Through the careful withholding of truth, in the slow drip of seduction and the dance of emotional power. Victory belongs not to the honest, but to the disciplined—to those who can control what they reveal, and weaponize what they withhold. This is their story—a journey into desire, control, obsession, fear, and ultimately, surrender. It is about what happens when illusions collide with truth, when strategies unravel, and when love, the most unpredictable battlefield of all, claims both victor and vanquished alike.

Proceed carefully, reader. This battlefield has no winners—only survivors.

Act One

Chapter One

The First Dance

"Choose carefully whom you bait, and never stir up the sharks."

-Robert Greene -48 Laws of Power

Chase

CHASE SANBOURNE HAD ALWAYS considered himself immune, a fifty-three-year-old divorcee with a daughter in her first year of college and a career as a Psychotherapist, that he was hoping to wind down and semi-retire to the Land of Smiles, a place that had been his refuge, playground, and dream for the last fifteen years following his divorce. He had come to love Phuket most of all, though he had been to Chiang Mai, Koh Samui, Bangkok of course, Hua Hin and Pattaya. Pattaya, the Devil's True Playground, and every die-hard Monger's Paradise was a bit too much for him. Besides the beer bars, Go-Go's and Gentleman's Clubs, there wasn't much of a beach scene and he liked to walk the beach during the days. No, Phuket had just the right balance for his long-term plans. Which had him, in his mind splitting his time in Chengdu, where he would live with Yuri, his girlfriend there, and Phuket, or so he had it worked out in his mind up to this point in his life.

Fifteen years of Thailand's rhythms had hardened him—or so he believed. He'd spent a lot of time in the beer bars, watched the Go-Go girls, and listened to the practiced lullabies of women who knew how to disarm a man with a touch and a glance. And he thought he could never be caught. Never be played.

He worked his two jobs back home, one as a psychologist in the role of mid-level bureaucrat, administrating care in a large system overseen by the government, and his evening job seeing clients in his practice, making good money and investing most of it to create passive streams of income to fuel his retirement dreams, while keeping two women in rotation. A Japanese woman, passionate and more than a little bit crazy, and a Philippina, rich but way too needy. Both vivacious, eager and always available, but not long-term keepers or so he thought to himself. No, he wasn't planning on settling down, and never thought he could get collared again.

Until he met Fern.

It was his third night in Phuket this trip, and already he had bar-hopped down Bangla Road with the jaded weariness of a veteran monger. But something about a particular side street pulled him in that night—a dark alley of neon heat and desperation. A strip of outdoor beer bars encircled by a dozen or so Go-Go Bars, where the air hung heavy with sweat, incense, and cheap perfume, and the girls in hordes who pulled at you to get you to stop and buy a drink and where the hawkers tried three at a time to steer you into their Go-Go for a "free look". As he ducked under the metal sign flashing the bar's name in bold red LEDs, he told himself through a wise assed grin "free to look". Stepping into the bar, one he had been too before but never thought to much of, as he had remembered it from his trip a year ago, and that's when he saw her.

Second girl from the left, as he moved to the center of the club and took a seat in the middle of the room.

She moved like she had studied movement—every sway calculated every glance sharp. Petite, slim, the kind of body that felt coiled tight and flexible. Her skin was pale for a Thai girl, and when she turned under the blue strobe, he could've sworn she looked Chinese. Or at least part-Chinese. Her small breasts barely moved under the thin bikini top, and her legs—those legs—were the perfect proportion for her height, toned from years of dancing, and just thick enough to appear healthy and give off the impression that she may be Chinese or Korean, just what he liked. She didn't look Thai, and did not have any tattoos or "the bar girl" look he had come to not like so much, after having spent years making the rounds in Pattaya, Bangkok and the lesser-known haunts in Thailand.

When their eyes met. She was already smiling, something she had trained herself to carry at all times she was on stage as she knew, regardless of how she felt on the inside, no-one liked a sad stripper, any more than they liked a mean one. She just looked at him like she was reading a book she'd already memorized, and knew instantly that he was interested in her. "Got One" she told herself as she put a bit more into her moves and the coyness in her smile.

The waitress informed her that he wanted to buy her a drink when she came off the stage. Before that, as he sipped his soda water, a short-haired dancer with a sly grin approached him—Fon, though he didn't know her name yet. She had a quickness in her eyes and the casual ease of someone who'd seen it all. She was accompanied by another girl, one with blonde hair woven into tight braids, both hardened looking Thai stripper types he thought, and neither one at all appealing.

"You like Fern?" Fon asked, her tone teasing.

Chase grinned. "She's... interesting."

Fon nudged her friend, who leaned over to join. "Buy my friend a drink, she no have customer yet tonight" Fon tested. Chase ignored the subtle beg, years in these types of bars, he knew the test when he heard it, see if the mark is a soft touch "Jai dee" or soft-hearted and if he was generous either by nature or by need. "So how much would it cost to keep her? You know, when I retire here. Live-in girlfriend, the whole package deal," he asked Fon, trying to appear as if he was half-joking, despite having already decided, in those few short minutes, that she was the one he wanted.

They shot each other a glance, whispered in Thai.

"Maybe... ninety thousand baht a month," Fon replied with mock seriousness. Her friend with the blond braids just nodded, pantomiming the fake seriousness for effect, both trying to look sincere and earnest as they sized up his reaction with calculated practice.

Chase didn't blink. "Seems fair. She'd be worth it." He replied, never giving away how absurd he knew the figure was, as he watched their reactions carefully, studying to see if they would give anything at all away about how much of a "Sucker" they thought he was.

He knew, through study and experience, that for the most part, Thai's at best tolerate the foreigner, and consider guys like him nothing more than walking ATMs. Resentment based on a host of factors, including but certainly not limited to racism, too many negative past experiences, and a grudging understanding that without men like him and their money, these women at least, would all be back in the villages farming rice or fucking Thai men for a fraction of what one of these white devils is willing to pay for a short-time stay.

The truth is, watching the hustle was what kept him coming back, the psychological games on full display like nowhere else, except perhaps on a prison yard. Thai hookers and convicted felons, master manip-ulators, the whole lot, and being in this environment honed his skills, or so he thought.

They both giggled, impressed by his poker face. Later that night, they'd tell Fern everything. Though the girls rarely, if ever talked about their customers, they did keep each other aware of a mark in the process of being flipped over onto his back, as they had each other's to the extent possible in this ruthless world.

Fern came to join him after her set. She sat next to him, close, bodies touching, but knew instinctively, with a guy like this, not to come on too strong, as guys like this were always turned off by the groping and pushy hard-sell type come-ons. "Where you from?" she asked, voice light but smooth, her English sharper than most, and her appearance innocent and demure, something she was practiced at and had honed, knowing that what she lacked in conventional beauty, she more than made up for in child-like innocence and sweetness.

"America," he answered.

"First time in Thailand?" she asked. Reading his responses with careful discreetness she too had perfected over the years.

He shook his head. "Not my first time." He responded, knowing the routine, the rehearsed questions all fired off in rapid fire succession, designed to quickly gauge how naïve and inexperienced a potential customer you might be. That combined with how you dressed put you into a set of simple categories all based on what your potential short-and-long-term value roughly meant to them.

They had a rating system, and a preferred "type", not due to personal preference or level of physical attraction, in that respect it was fairly cut and dried, they almost invariably preferred, hot, fit, young Thai men, but when it came to customers, they wanted them fat, old, and rich, and Asian, Japanese, Korean, or Chinese, one of the rich developed nations in Asia, and then the Westerners, *Farang*, loosely translate meant "*Whitey*", and in most circles it was not a term of endearment, but a slur. Then at the bottom of the scale were Indians and Blacks, for what most don't see through the abundance of smiles in Thailand, is that the darker your skin, the less attractive you are to them. That and the Indians were notorious for their strong body odor, something Thais, who as a rule are fastidious with their hygiene, loathe as a matter of fact.

"Ahh…" Her smile didn't falter. "But you still come back."

"That interests you.?" He asked, realizing that she was smarter than most, as she didn't follow her first question with what ninety-five percent of the others would have asked, which would have been, "how long your holiday?", the second questioned designed to determine if you might become a customer, how long they had to work on you to get you into the ultimate position, that of long-time sponsor. A rapid-fire series of questions, seemingly innocent, innocuous, casually friendly, but all designed to determine if you were only going to buy them a drink or two, take them for a short-time or long-time screw, or potentially set them up with a regular monthly stipend.

In other words, and nothing else, how much were you potentially worth too them financially. That's it, nothing friendly about it no matter how convincing they appeared, and the good ones, could make you really believe they gave a fuck. But the truth was, it was all an illusion, they were at work, and their job was to extract as much from you as possible. That must never be forgotten he reminded himself quickly, as he found himself being drawn to her physically which wasn't that unusual, but intellectually as well, which was very rare. Her ability to pivot instinctually from the script of routine questions by itself, set her apart, but there was more, and he couldn't put his finger on that yet, but it was alluring, and he couldn't take his eyes off of her.

Fern

She didn't think anything of him the first or second night he came back to the club to see her, but when he came back three nights in a row. Different times. Different moods. But always the same table. And always for *her*, she knew for sure she had a live one on her hands. For all intents and purposes, he was nothing to get excited about, handsome perhaps to some's standards years ago, but now just aging and trying like most, not to show it.

She noticed how he dressed—no tourist tank tops or sandals. He wore collared linen shirts, pressed slacks, and expensive watches. Never the same pair of shoes twice. That said something. Maybe pride. Maybe wealth. Probably both, but almost assuredly, an underlying insecurity, masking his lack of a sense of real self-worth. She had seen it all so many times before, recognizing it had become automatic, and knowing how to leverage it was routine. She understood the route to take with him. He would be her "superman".

He didn't paw her like the others, in fact seemed less interested in groping her body than in probing her mind by hearing what she had to say. He didn't ask crude questions. He listened, and stared into her eyes, always speaking slowly and saying little, but listening intently. That made her wary.

After a while, they would fall into a rhythm. Making out at the table, kissing deeply, like lovers in a movie. She pressed herself into him during her breaks, danced in his lap, ground on him until he wrapped his arms around her and held her tightly against him, firm but gently. She noticed that he didn't seem anxious with the physicality, the illusion of intimacy, or the public display, like he could tune out the rest of the world and be present with just her. He was sensual, experienced, and comfortable with a woman, not awkward or clumsy like many of the men she dealt with regularly, and he knew how to kiss.

He only asked what the bar-fine would be and listened as she pointed out how the red ribbon tied to her bikini meant she had to go with customers if they asked, but when she said the bar fine was the ridiculous amount: 10,000 Baht, she gauged his response and followed up with, they make it that high early in the evenings to keep the girls in the club. "If everyone leave, and bar has no dancers, customer won't stay and drink." While he knew that was a bullshit line some girls told to keep from going out with guys they didn't want to fuck, he nodded understandably and never even hinted at it again with her.

He quickly wondered to himself, if her bullshit line was because he was just another old farang, gross and disgusting in her eyes, or if there might be some legitimacy to it, as he had always thought girls like this loved to go as many short-times as possible, and could cover 4 to 5 men in a night, all while returning to the bar and making commissions from drinks in between. It was a win-win for them and the bar which charged a fee, the bar-fine, to each customer that took a lady out no matter how long the stay lasted.

That was unusual. That was interesting, most guys that put in that much time with her, wanted to take her out for at least a short-time, if they really liked her, she could parlay that into a week on one of the islands, or as much as a live-in two-week trip in Chengdu or Tokyo, or Seoul. Though as she got older, those customers were fewer and further between, and she couldn't ignore that reality as hard as she tried.

She had sized him up, and determined, the best approach was to let him set the pace, create tension by not selling herself quickly, as he had already demonstrated interest by coming back and not pushing hard, that represented investment, which she understood meant leverage. Another angle, and one she intended to apply.

"Spit your drink in my mouth," she whispered more than once, her lips brushing against his. He hesitated. Then complied. Confused. Excited. Repulsed. She could read it all on his face. She liked watching him flinch, seeing him fall under her control. She knew that creating simultaneously conflicting feelings had the combined effect of increasing attraction and commitment to her in ways most men had no idea about. She was anchoring him to her like she had done so many times before with the others, finding each one's line to cross was part of her work.

She didn't like the men she manipulated, but she loved how good she had gotten at it, and would tell herself things like "it was all part of the mission" as if she was a spy on some covert espionage operation, anything more than what she really was. All part of the fairy tale illusions she wrapped herself in to insulate herself from the cruel and inevitable passing of time and the reality that she was heading towards a bleak and lonely future. The control she believed she obtained was real, in her mind, and who needed love when being in control felt so much safer.

And he came back, like she knew he would. He was mentally weak for her and she sensed it, she loved it. It fueled her, and besides, this was after all her life's blood, and what had become her life's work. She ignored the fact that she didn't have much else, no car, no house, no children, nothing 'but the next mission" chasing money so she could send it home and garner some approval and validation from her mother, and hopefully her name on the deed to the house she was paying the lion's share of the mortgage on. She was frugal, saved everything else, and had ways to invest so that one day, when time finally caught up to her, she would be safe, maybe not well off, but okay financially.

Each night after their encounters, she filed away details for later—his tastes, his tells, his weaknesses. She'd done this for years. Her handlers and the other girls over the years had taught her how to catalog men, predict their patterns. But there was something about him. Something she couldn't quite sort yet.

Fon teased her. "You gonna keep him?" she asked as they sat slurping beef noodle soup at Pom's Noodle Bar, a side stall off of Second Road after their shift, neither one having been bar fined that night, or the last few nights for that matter.

"Who she asked," pretending not know who Fon was referring too. "The Old White Farang, the rich one" Fon stated. Fern rolled her eyes. "Let's see if he lasts the week. He's got the money, but he's trickier than most, and thinks he's smarter than he is," and they both had a laugh as they went back to texting their regular sponsors, work never ended it seemed.

Pom the old lady running the noodle stand, a former working girl herself, took it all in, a theme she had lived herself in her past life and a drama she continued to watch unfold night after night as the next generation played it now. She had gotten to know Fern well over the past few years, the younger often coming to her stall alone, when she had something on her mind, and would seek support and wisdom from the old woman, who had come to see her as a younger version of herself.

Chase (continued)

One night, between her sets, while she nuzzled into him like a kitten pretending to be drunk, smelling his skin as she kissed him "Thai" style, he spoke the words out loud.

"I'm thinking of moving here. In three years. When I retire."

Fern paused, then stated, "You retire young?"

"I have a pension, and only have to work for twenty years, and I can consult remotely in anyplace that has a good internet connection."

She blinked slowly, registering it. He expected her to be impressed. Instead, she smiled faintly and rested her cheek against his shoulder. "Wow" she stated with that practiced innocence you might expect from an eight-year-old who had just had a magician pull a quarter out from behind her ear. Her voice, practiced, lithe and childlike, faking a sense of wonderment to create a sense of feigned awe that her customers always took as flattering, as if she was somehow in awe and impressed all at once. It had an effect, that she knew was as powerful as it was disarming.

He had spotted the move the first time she had employed it, now he was sure, it was a part of her routine. His analysis of her was slowly coming into view, she appeared to be the classic *Puella Eterna*, in Jungian terms, the perpetual woman-child, the archetypal image of the woman who refused, though unconsciously, to ever grow up and assume a true adult life, instead opting, though largely unaware to live in a fairy tale world of romanticism and fantasy, or at least that was his hunch. He was certainly sure she was using innocence to compensate for a lack of conventional beauty, and he found her ability to do so a reflection of her intelligence and adaptability.

While he hated to admit it, he respected her for her intelligence and ability to overcome what would, particularly in the career she had chosen or been thrust into, other-wise be a liability. Like the ugly fish, who assumes a role to attract its prey, rather than using speed, attractive colors, or agility to capture its next meal. She used the illusion of innocence and a sweet, almost childlike wonderment to disarm.

"You serious?" She asked. "Dead serious." Was his reply. Typical of him, short and direct and lacking in much embellishment.

That night, when she walked away for her next set, he thought about what he was really saying. He had a house back home, a daughter in college, a business bringing in good money. The plan was to cash out, take his pension, and disappear into the heat and chaos of Thailand, working some if he felt like it, or not. Cheap drinks. Quiet beaches. A woman like Fern. Was that what he was selling to her, future faking her, or himself? And how had she somehow, in his mind, worked her way into the equation so quickly he asked himself.

He didn't know yet what he was really asking for. He just knew he didn't want to spend the rest of his life tied to the government's bureaucratic cluster fuck of a machine, and seeing if he could get this girl to go with him, and not be her customer, was it really possible? Was he that good, that delusional, or just that stupid? Or was it something darker, more related to his Shadow than he was presently aware of? Were the psychological dynamics she was displaying mirroring his own? Or was he trying to level up his game? Control the mind of a stripper, slip past the professional persona, which as a rule was strong, and pull her into his frame? Or all of it?

That had to be what it was, her shadow, mirrored his, and drew him to her in ways he would only come to understand later, and probably far too late. After all, at his age, and still bumming around SEA, adventure seeking, rather than building a family, and strong ties to his professional and social communities, perhaps Chase was like her, simply not wanting to grow up either. He had never cared about social status or with moving up through the ranks at his job. He wanted adventure, the thrill of what may lie around the next bend in the road, the intoxication of a new romance, anything but the mundane drudgery that existed in the day-to-day life of a bureaucrat.

Still, he also wanted something warm. Real. And maybe fake-real would do just fine. After all, the way he had grown up had trained him to live in a world of illusion where love, real love was as evasive as a handful of smoke. And now that was exactly what he was trying to do, cup handfuls of smoke, and then look to see if when he opened his hands, there was anything actually there, it was a game he had played as a child, and now as an adult, he found that he was still playing it.

She smiled to herself as she listened to him talk about his life back home, knowing that she didn't have to say anything, in fact, should say as little as possible. Just let them talk, and appear interested, and impressed. That's what most of these guys, and she didn't think he was any different, actually wanted. To be heard and thought of as impressive, as pathetic as it was, it was really that simple.

Fern

She watched him leave again that night. Another sudden exit. Always just after the start of her next set. He never stayed too late either, maybe an hour and a half or two tops. Never lingered to see what other men might do, or what she might do with them for a drink or two, and he never got drunk or sloppy. Sometimes, he would nod in her direction as he sauntered towards the door, and sometimes he wouldn't, he would just walk out, not looking back at her or even in her direction. Few men ever did that, at least not any of the ones who she thought were interested in her. She knew what he was doing however and that intrigued her, because it meant that he was trying, and that meant opportunity.

Later that night, towards the end of her shift, and before the club closed, she stood in the back with Fon after her final rotation, applying lipstick in the mirror under flickering fluorescent lights.

"He said he wants to move here," Fern said casually. Fon smirked. "I told you he was one of those."

"Three years, he has a pension and is in some kind of work that he can do remotely online and get paid for it."

Fon lit a cigarette. "So? You going to make him your sponsor?" She chided, though completely serious.

Fern didn't answer. She just stared at her reflection. Then tightened the strap a bit on her bikini top, and checked herself again in the mirror.

"I think he's testing me," she said.

Fon raised an eyebrow and laughed and simply stated "Dumb Farang."

Patong by day was a different world. The Go-Go bars were closed, shutters pulled down. Stray dogs roamed past massage parlors, half feral cats crept in corners, and the men were either nursing hangovers or would resume drinking beer in the beer bars along Bangla Road when they reopened in a few hours. In the early morning, street vendors hosed down the sidewalks, ladyboys hung in small packs hoping for a short-time customer, and the bargirls who were homeless and hadn't earned enough from the night before to afford a cheap room, sat together drinking beer and trying to make the best of their situation before giving it another go later that night. Hungover tourists in tank tops wandered aimlessly, sunburned and dazed.

And the girls, the dancers, the hunters, slept like vampires behind blackout curtains.

But Fern was always awake by noon. She messaged her sponsors, something she had trained herself through discipline to do as a part of her routine. She knew through experience that most of these men led boring lives back home and getting frequent messages with sugary sweet words kept them hooked. She did all this while checking her crypto wallet, getting a massage or her hair done, or watching news or movies on her phone in the room she shared with five other dancers, while she ate sticky rice with grilled pork. And she thought.

Chase had potential. He was dangerous. Not because he could hurt her. But because he might mean something. She hated that thought. But it crept in anyway. She had to get the hook in a bit deeper, but the next move was his, and if she had played the game as well as she knew she had, she knew exactly what he would do.

Chapter Two

The Dance Deepens

THE NEXT FEW DAYS melted together in a strange, half-lucid haze of sun, heat, and late-night neon. Chase found himself living for the moments between 9 p.m. and 12 a.m., when she'd be on her set rotation and then, if he was lucky, not with another customer, but instead, sliding into his lap, her skin slick with coconut oil and sweat, eyes bright and unreadable, her smile alive, innocent, and childlike.

The hours outside the club dragged on longer than he cared to admit, and what's more, he knew he was engaging in some world class rationalization. To try and combat the abyss, he knew he was diving into head first, he developed a series of mantras he would try and repeat to himself over and over throughout the day:

"You are not special; you are a mark if you let yourself be."

"Your girl isn't different," and, the harshest and most true of all, the one that was undeniable, and unavoidable:

"She's a hooker!"

He found himself repeating these over and over to himself, and then telling himself that he didn't care, that "he was training himself to recognize feelings and not let them control him." But he was failing, as he was allowing a sick and twisted form of psychotic logic override, the truth he knew to be - she was a hooker and he was a mark to her. That was it, period. Nevertheless, he thought he could stay in control and, perhaps, that was the greatest delusion of all, that he in fact was ever really in control.

He tried to keep busy during the day. Morning walks on the beach, sweating through his shirt before 9 a.m. The air in Patong never cooled, only changed flavors—ocean salt, fish sauce, diesel exhaust, the occasional pungent odor of marijuana smoke. He hit the gym once a day, working out like a savage, harder than he ever did back at home. Scooter rides around the island, exploring different areas, which is how he discovered Rawai Beach, or he would get a Thai massage, yet he still couldn't relax.

His mind remained fixed on her.

They didn't exchange numbers. There were no messages. No morning-after texts or cutesy emoji-studded updates. Their world only existed inside the club, under blacklight and spotlights, between rotations and overpriced drinks. It was entirely her world, her domain, and he was just a visitor, a novice, someone so far out of his depth that he couldn't even realize or understand the complexities of the operations around him, and that was just the way she liked it.

And still, he thought of her constantly.

He tried to remind himself of the rule—the unspoken law shared by every jaded monger in every dark expat bar.

Three days. No more than three nights with the same girl. Any longer and you could lose control. You mistake the show for something real. You start building castles on a beach that only exists after sunset.

But this was night four.

And he was still going back. That part was a foregone conclusion, and while he always felt like a chump slinking back behind the curtain, sure the hawkers in front and the doormen were now in on it, snickering to themselves as they pantomimed feigned "respect" for the repeat customer, they all knew and were in on the hustle. He was Fern's mark, her property, and they knew the longer he kept coming back, the more that was in it for them. Hell, one or more of them was probably fucking her on the side. Who knows? One could be a Thai boyfriend or even her husband. Guys like Chase would never know the truth, or even a part of it, not until it was way too late.

Fern

She didn't understand it.

She had other customers. A few of them. Some older, some richer, some louder. A Norwegian guy who liked her feet. An Aussie who always tried to kiss her neck and tickle her. A Korean sponsor who sent her money every week in exchange for blurry topless videos and pet names. Those where the one's she kept in regular daily contact with and from whom she could either expect a regular monthly stipend, or whom she could reach out to if she needed money for something, which she always found a reason to ask for every so often, not too often, but often enough.

In addition to her salary from pushing drinks in the bar, and going both short and long-time with customers, and the income she was generating from all of her sponsors combined to equal about 90,000 baht. That when combined with her salary, put her income in the highest bracket in Thailand, exceeding what most doctors and professionals made and far above what she would otherwise earn with her education and skillset in any other profession. But she knew her window of opportunity was closing fast and she wanted a way out, a soft landing, something she could ease into and then rest.

But none of them got to her like Chase did.

It wasn't that he was better looking, though he was. It wasn't that he was kinder, though he was that, too. It was the way he made her feel seen—not as a body, but as a person. As something deeper.

That was dangerous.

And yet, each evening as she walked into the club, makeup set and hair done up, she found herself wondering if he'd show up again. She'd either see him walk in, or would look up and see him in his customary spot, watching and waiting. The familiar tailored shirts. That strange quiet intensity. Those damn nice shoes.

Fon teased her. "You checking the clock again? He's got you."

Fern scoffed, "I'm just trying to hit my drink quota."

But Fon saw through it. And she resented her for showing too much interest, a threat to her, and him for having the ability to impact

Fern that way, to distract her away from her. She seethed and began thinking about how she should proceed, as she couldn't let this get too far.

Fern carried out her routines during the day—market trips, laundry, hair appointments, bank transfers to her mother, feeding the handful of semi feral cats that hung around the alley behind the club. But the thought of Chase stayed with her, like a faint hum just beneath the noise.

And she hated that.

She couldn't afford to like someone. Not in the real sense. Her life was designed around survival. Her handlers and friends had drilled that into her. Get in. Get what you need. Get out or string them along. Maintain the illusion, at all costs, keep the fantasy alive, milking as much as you can for as long as you can, without ever giving away anything, nothing real, dignity having been exchanged for cash, that was the deal she had made when she entered this life, and she could not afford to forget it now.

And yet...

She caught herself hoping he'd come.

Chase

They were sitting together again that night between her sets. Her perfume was light—lemongrass, maybe. Something clean. He liked that. She pressed against him gently as he sipped his club soda and traced lazy circles on her thigh and around her ankle. He also like the way her body felt sleek with a thin layer of sweat right after stepping off stage, skin cool and tight but soft, and how she felt in his arms, like she was supposed to be there.

"You said you liked math," he said. Fern smiled. "I like problems with answers." He grinned. "Ever considered teaching?"

Her face hardened for just a second—so quick he wouldn't have caught it if he hadn't been watching. Then she softened again and leaned in close. There was something there she didn't want to talk about he thought, but he couldn't imagine what it could be. Had she thought about a career in teaching, had she had a problem in school when she was younger, he couldn't guess.

"Maybe. When I'm old." "You're not that young," he said, teasing. "Neither are you," she shot back. They laughed. Then kissed again. Harder this time. A dance between hunger and performance.

As they parted, she slid his finger into his drink, then pushed it all the way into her mouth and down the back of her throat without gagging. All the while watching the look on his face, measuring his reaction. Then came the line she whispered each night, but always like it was the first time.

"Spit your drink in my mouth."

This time, he paused longer. "Why do you like that?"

She smiled without blinking. "Because you don't."

It was her way of trying to own him. And maybe, he thought, she already did.

Back at Their Distance

They had no way of reaching each other outside the club. There were no calls. No text history. Just presence and absence.

During the day, Fern drifted through her errands thinking about him in flashes. A smell at the fresh market that reminded her of his aftershave. A man walking past in a linen shirt that made her pulse skip until she saw it wasn't him.

Chase, in turn, kept waiting for the moment the spell would break. He jotted in his notebook like he had back in school. But now, instead of case notes, it was fragments.

"Four nights. Three-day rule broken. What does that make me?"

"Do they teach them to kiss like that?"

"If she looked for me, even once... what did that mean?"

And, the one he knew was the most important of all, "Your girl isn't different, and neither are you!"

He tried to step back perceptually, and put things in the correct and proper context. When he was in the club, they were together, if she wasn't already with another customer when he got there. She wasn't waiting for him, she was available to him, if he was there because he paid to buy her drinks which helped her meet her quota and earn a living, and when he wasn't there, she was with whomever, as many as possible, doing exactly what she was doing with him each night with them.

Playing the same role, the same coquettish games, running the same hustle, trying her best to make them feel as special and as important as she was with him. Night after night, customer after customer. There was no way she was "his girl". The idea was so patently ridiculous he couldn't believe how stupid he felt even having to remind himself of it.

And yet, he went back, at this point he had to, he had invested too much and wanted too much, regardless of how absurd and foolish it all started to become. One night, he had caught a glimpse of it, as Fern stood up from his lap to return to the stage to start her set, a girl on the stage in the middle of her own set made eye contact with him and smirked, shook her head and looked away.

The look said it all, "sucker," "she's got you," "poor bastard doesn't realize she was giving a blowjob in the VIP room two hours before he got there." Whatever. The look said all of that and more, and he knew it, but he didn't care. He rationalized that he could get her to fall for him, that with enough time, he could get her to want him the way he wanted her. He marveled at how the feeling was the same, a regular girlfriend in his arms, or a professional, to him, it felt the same, so he moved forward in a direction he knew deep down inside was only going to lead to one place.

That night, as she nestled beside him at their usual seat on the couch, just before the song change signaling the start for the next set, he reached into his shirt pocket and pulled out a small, precisely folded slip of paper.

He looked at her, not as a customer. Not as a man ready to pay.

"I *want* to see you," he said softly. "Not here. If you're interested and have the time available."

He pressed the note into her hand. "My WhatsApp. Just... if you're available."

Then he stood, slowly, and without waiting for her reaction, walked toward the exit. The lights shifted pink and blue behind him, casting long shadows that seemed to follow him out.

Fern sat still. She didn't open the paper. Not yet. Not in front of the other girls. Not under the cameras.

But his word echoed. Want.

Not buy.

Want.

While that was dangerous, it also meant she had him right where she wanted, everything according to plan, as expected, except it wasn't.

Chapter Three

Off Script

"Always say less than necessary."
-Robert Greene, The 48 Laws of Power

Chase

He didn't expect her to message him. Not really. A part of him hoped she wouldn't. It would make things easier. He could take it as a sign, a graceful out, proof that he was imagining too much in their brief collision of glances and kisses. He could walk away with his pride a bit bruised, but still fully intact.

But another part of him, a bigger part, knew better. She wasn't the type to let a mark like him wander off without something real in return. These girls knew how to work a long hustle and understood that to do so right, time had to be invested. It was exactly that, an investment with an anticipated rate of return. Nothing was ever free in places like this and certainly not with a girl like Fern.

So, when the message lit up his screen at 10:42 a.m. the next morning, he stared at it longer than he should have.

Fern: Hi, did I wake you up? I no disturb your sleep, Kha?" A minute later: "You free today? My day off."

He smiled at the screen, thumb hesitating. Then he responded, "Yeah, you want to get dinner together? I can pick you up."

She responded with "6 p.m. you pick me up at police station, ok?" She was surprised when he asked, "the one next to the Khon Kean BBQ on Second Road?" Most Farang never made if off Beach and Bangla Road, at least not the well-polished ones like Chase, or so she thought to herself. "No" she responded, "the one at the end of Bangla on Beach Road." His response was a simple "Ok, see you then."

Why did she expect more from him in that moment, he seemed like he could have taken or left the situation without an actual date. He wasn't trying to qualify himself to her, didn't boast about some fancy place he wanted to take her to in order to try and impress her, never mentioned that he was excited to see her. None of the typical things she was used to getting from the men who pursued her. She made note.

She had just stepped out of the shower when her phone buzzed. She didn't want to admit it to herself, but as she reached for the phone she wondered, hoped even, that it was a message from him. And when she saw it was from his WhatsApp address, her heart skipped a beat.

She smiled to herself when she read the message, not because he wanted to see her, but because she knew she was in control. She quickly gauged his having waited a day to reach out as nothing more than a novice's attempt to appear aloof, and it made her smile to know how hard he was trying to play it cool. She had him on the hook and enjoyed the tug on the end of the line. It felt like opportunity, profit, easy money.

But the something else she felt, the thing she wanted to ignore, was what stuck in her mind and made her think twice about how she should be proceeding. She was upset with herself for letting him know so much about her life and her schedule. Why did she want him to know she had that much time available? Was she hoping he wanted more than just dinner or a drink? She convinced herself that she was just trying to set him up to ask if he could long-time her for a GFE during her day off so she could turn it into a profitable one, but she knew that wasn't the whole truth.

Chase wrote "Wear something casual, we're going on the motorcycle."

She never let a man see where she lived. That was a hard and fast rule. So, when she told Chase to meet her at the police box just off Beach Road at the end of Bangla, she wasn't being mysterious. Just cautious.

He was waiting when she got there. Standing just off to the side of the police box where Bangla spat itself into the sea, looking half-tourist, half-professor in a linen shirt and sandals, his thinning hair combed back like he was trying to convince someone, maybe himself, that he still had it. He had a bottle of cold water in one hand, and his phone in the other, checking it like he was pretending not to wait for her.

She saw him before he saw her. Watched him for a few seconds. He didn't fidget like most men did. He stood still. That meant something. Maybe patience. Maybe control. Or maybe, she thought with a flicker of a smile, he was just too old to pace around in the heat.

She made sure to approach with a small bounce in her step, the same energy she used on stage, toned down just enough to suggest she was off-duty, but still worth every second of his time. He looked up and smiled, the kind of smile that men wore when they thought something was about to happen. And it was, of course. Just not what he expected.

"Wow," he said, echoing her line, and mimicking the shoulder shrug and facial expression she always used when deploying it for exaggerated effect and enhanced cuteness.

She tilted her head slightly, not breaking her stride. "You stealing my word now?"

He laughed, a low, quiet sound that didn't quite match the beach noise or the swarm of tourists waddling by. He was nervous, but he was trying not to be. That made him interesting. Most guys either drooled or barked commands. Chase walked some strange line between believing he was in control and knowing he wasn't.

She had expected him to have a plan. A farang always had a plan she thought. But when she asked where they were going, he just shrugged and said, "We'll see." He didn't say it like someone who didn't care. He said it like someone who wanted to let the night unfold, not choreograph it. That made her uneasy. And curious.

"We have to walk to my hotel and get the bike he said" and she thought, *here it comes*. But when they got to the front of his hotel, he simply nodded to the saluting security guard as he opened the seat to his scooter and handed her a helmet. No awkward invitation to go quickly to his room to "pick something up he had forgotten" before the ungraceful attempt to make his move to bed her. Instead, he just said "jump on and hold on tight."

They rode aimlessly for a while, weaving through the traffic of beach-bound scooters and roadside stalls. He pulled into a fancy restaurant overlooking the ocean on the hill heading out of Patong toward Kamala. It was clearly expensive, with a host at the front in a tailored white shirt.

"Reservation only," the host said politely. "We're full tonight."

Chase smiled. "No problem." Then he turned to Fern. "We'll figure this out. Let's roll."

No flinch. No frustration. Just motion. He didn't argue, protest or appear upset or rattled in any way like most Western men typically did in this type of situation when they were used to getting what they wanted, when they wanted it, and without ever being told No, and that registered with her.

Instead, he repeated the line for her to "hop on and hold on tight" as he headed them back towards Patong. About a half a mile or so later, he pulled into a place called the Salty Duck Café, a much less ostentatious outdoor roadside restaurant specializing in Isaan food. She smiled as she dismounted. "Isaan restaurant. Like where I'm from, Khon Kaen."

He looked pleased. "Thought it looked right."

They shared grilled chicken wings, spicy Tom Yum, and sticky rice and drank Cokes. He was trying not to sweat, as the heat of the evening was getting to him, but he ignored it and watched her as she ate. He didn't talk a lot and didn't say much when he did. She looked down at her food mostly and while she wasn't nervous at all, she tried to appear as if she was, knowing that would disarm him and put him more at ease. Still, she was mildly surprised that he didn't ramble on incessantly like most of the men that took her out seemed to do, either trying to qualify themselves or seek her approval for how affluent they thought they were, bragging about their jobs, house, car, or whatever they thought she might think was important. He just chewed slowly and appeared to study her. He didn't need to interrupt the silence to feel comfortable, and when he did speak, it was measured, calm, and he looked her in the eye.

After dinner, he drove them up to Kamala to a quiet strip of beach bars. It was a place a bit off the beaten path few tourists knew. A row of hidden bars and beach-facing tables just off a narrow, dark road. They walked along the path that separated the bars and restaurants from the beach, under the moonlight, their conversation light at first, then deeper.

He told her about his work, his clinic, the job with the government, his plan to retire in three years. She pointed out the vines that hung from the trees they walked under and made note of how he kept himself between her and the traffic as they turned off the path and onto the road leading to some small bars. She felt protected. He indicated that he too liked the vines, and noticed how they shared a smile in that moment, having connected over something so random.

They took a seat in a nondescript beer bar and sat opposite each other at a small table along the front of the bar immediately next to the road. When he mentioned his pension, he noticed something shift in her expression. A flicker, brief but sharp. He couldn't tell if it was resentment, jealousy, greed, or something else entirely. But he made a note in his mind, and reminded himself not to brag, boast or appear too full of himself. He knew that arrogance and to brag was unattractive in any culture, but especially those in SEA, and he didn't want to appear as if he was trying to impress her, even though he wanted to sell her on a view of a future together, one that was stable and secure.

He also knew that the less he said, the better, yet he had to resist the urge to try and sell himself to her and made note of the fact that he had to be deliberate with this intent. Of all the women in his life, why should he care at all what *she* thought of him. Clearly, obviously, here, in this situation, it was he who had everything to offer, and she, nothing more than what he could have already bought for a few US dollars if he wanted it, but that wasn't entirely true, and he wasn't sure why. He reflected later and decided that it had been so long since he had been in the company of a woman whose thoughts he cared to know that he wondered if he was putting her on the proverbial pedestal and what a trap that was for both of them.

While he knew he had a lot to offer, and knew she knew it too, he didn't know yet if she actually cared, and what's more he wasn't sure why he seemed to, and that was bothering him. He was making another mistake and he resented himself for it as quickly as he realized what it was. He was starting to like her, and that was a big mistake in any setting, but here in Thailand, with a working girl, it was potentially disastrous. Truly liking one of these girls makes them more than just someone you are interested in casually or one you want to sleep with. She was now more than a commodity. She was a person.

The bar had a Connect Four set on a nearby table. When he invited her to play, she feigned ignorance.

"You ever play?" he asked.

She shook her head. "No. What is it?"

"Really?"

Too innocent.

He explained quickly. She caught on fast. Too fast.

"You sure you've never played?"

"It's a simple formula" she casually explained despite appearing to have no prior knowledge of the game, and after winning their third or fourth match, he realized she was far more intelligent than he had appreciated earlier, and either way, if she knew how to play or not, her grasping that there was a simple straightforward way to almost ensure victory impressed him. It wasn't just that the concept was intuitive to her, it was how casually she acknowledged it, as if it was so simply obvious it didn't deserve mention. He was almost certain it was not part of her ruse, and if it was, it was expert. He was impressed.

She was practiced in letting the Farang talk about themselves, their lives, their careers, possessions, whatever. Most couldn't help but brag and make the entire conversation about themselves. She had gotten good at nodding and acting impressed, easily hiding both her boredom and disdain, and at times outright contempt. After so many years, it had gotten easy. Just smile, look impressed, and every once in a while, pull out her well-used and rehearsed "Wow," eyes wide and face expressive. They always fell for it. It was too easy. They were too self-absorbed and stupid to notice, or care.

Most were just trying to pass enough time pretending they were interested in anything more than a fast screw to assuage their own sense of Western morality. Those that still clung to whatever semblance of innocence that remained despite finding themselves in the world's largest brothel, and certainly by design, not accident, that they chose places like this for their holidays, some even dragging their families along to further the charade and self-delusion. But for some reason, he seemed different, and she wasn't exactly sure how or why.

Sure, he talked too much about himself, after all, he was a farang. But there were too many times when he appeared genuinely interested in her, her life, her past, her dreams, or what she thought. Or he would sit quietly, observing her, seeming to wait for her to break the silence. Comfortable with the quiet between them, and not easily moved by the natural tension it created. The worst was when he commented on something he noticed about her. Traits, qualities, little things she valued about herself that most men, especially customers, never saw. That worried her. She couldn't let him get that close.

There was something else about him that she was trying to discern. It appeared when he would stare off momentarily, murmuring the lines to some slow sad song that played casually in the background. Thais were naturally sentimental as well, but his reaction almost seemed wounded, broken, too heartfelt and to distracting. She saw another in, and planned to exploit it when the time presented itself. He was heartbroken, she realized, and while she didn't know why or how, she knew that made it easier for her, and she smiled to herself like a player in a game who just pulled further ahead of their opponent. "Poor baby" she thought to herself, "it's about to get so much worse for you, if your little heart is hurting now, just wait." She was vacillating, between something akin to interest, and pure predation.

He noticed she saw his romantic heart shine through, and the pained look he allowed to show while murmuring the lyrics to a sad Eagles tune about a man who couldn't let himself be loved. Most women never picked up on it. She was clearly different, and he was sure nothing got past her.

The Billiard Curveball

He told her he wanted to shoot some pool and said they should head back to Patong. As they rode back through the cool night air, she held him around the waist tighter than she needed to. The smell of his skin, the breeze, the speed at which he drove. It stirred something in her she hadn't felt in a long time.

When they parked the scooter near his hotel, she waited for the inevitable invitation to his room. Some ridiculous pretext, like wanting to pick something up, or a need to change his shirt. But it never came. Instead, he led her down Beach Road, cut up a side street, turned down Second Road and as they ran across the street and ducked into a small soi filled with bars, she became aware that this would represent the third or fourth place they had been too in one night.

So, she thought, *he was trying to increase the perceived closeness and familiarity she would feel developing between them through the creation of discreet and distinct memories in a short period of time.* She became aware that he was trying to get past her professional persona and get close emotionally to her personally, and she recalibrated slightly in response to the new realization. She appreciated the level of effort he was making for her even if his moves were transparent. He was different and, on another level, than most of the men she dealt with, and she respected that about him while at the same time seeing that in a very real way he was making it so easy for her. *When your prey is heading straight towards you, just stand still and let them come,* she thought to herself.

He ordered drinks and started a game of pool with one of the bargirls. Fern had told him earlier she didn't know how to play, but wouldn't mind if he did while she watched. She knew to always go along with what the "customer" wanted, no matter how obscene, offensive, degrading, or disgusting, and while watching him shoot pool may be boring, it certainly wasn't any of the others.

The girl was from Isaan—Khon Kaen, like her. Fernn struck up a conversation with the others at the bar. As they talked in Thai, she found out the girl Chase was playing with was heading back to her village the next day for a holiday, or at least that is what she told him. She noticed the way he looked at her, appreciating the thickness of her thighs and the way she moved and how her curves popped when she bent over the table to take her shots, even though he tried to be discrete, his "type" was becoming clear to her, and she herself fit the bill almost perfectly.

"She from near me," Fern said, approaching him casually. "Going home tomorrow. If you like her, you could pay bar-fine, take her. Help her out. Give her extra for her trip, nice bonus to help her travel and holiday."

It came out so easily. Casually. But she watched him closely. She had decided she wanted to test him to see how he would respond.

Chase was taken aback. Despite finding the girl attractive, the suggestion hit like a mild gut punch. Her casual tone turned him into a commodity. He masked the sting, but barely.

"I wouldn't disrespect you like that," he said. "We came together, and I always go home with the girl I brought to the dance." He wasn't even sure she'd get the idiom, but it was all he had, and he was surprised that he had been caught off guard and flat footed by her test, only recognizing it for what it was moments after she had delivered it. That too bothered him because it meant that he was starting to like her more than he wanted to, which meant she was beating him, something he really wasn't ready to admit. And if it was something else, her just jerking his emotional strings, he obviously didn't like that either.

She smiled coolly. "I don't mind. It would help her. She like sister."

He brushed it off. Tried to stay cool. But he made a note. Her voice, her posture—everything changed when talking to the other girls. It was a chink in her armor. The first real one, besides her too well rehearsed childlike wonderment ploy with the word "Wow". He realized she was testing him, and while he thought he remained unrattled, he knew he could have handled the situation far better than he had.

What he should have said was something along the lines of "Sure, we can bar fine her together if that's your thing baby," and gave her a playful wink, but the truth was, he liked her too much and as a result was too afraid to possibly offend her. He cringed when realizing how pathetically he had handled the situation and even more so about how he was starting to feel.

Imagining offending a Thai hooker by being flirtatious and a bit provocative, later made him feel all the more ridiculous and resentful of how badly he was losing this game. The fact that it may have been over well before he ever realized it, like the winning chess player seeing the inevitable victory in x number of moves, he hadn't yet realized he was likely beaten. She on the other hand had never been in doubt, at all times she felt in full control, almost.

The bar had to stop selling alcohol at midnight, some obscure Thai holiday or something or the other, yet they stayed open, not being able to afford kicking out paying customers so they just pulled the metal curtains down and asked everyone to keep their voices down in case the police decided to make their rounds. Laws in Thailand always seemed to Chase, to be taken by the locals to be like suggestions that could easily be ignored if it meant extracting money from tourists.

By then Chase had switched from drinking soda water with lime to Sang Som and Cola, and as the alcohol began to set in, she noticed him becoming more relaxed and freer with his money. *So, he was farang after all*, she mused to herself, as he tried to beat every girl in the bar at connect four and succeeding several times in a row with two of the younger, newer, less experienced girls, and becoming a bit too proud of himself in the process. Still, she acknowledged to herself that his boyishness with his guard down was cuter than she wanted to admit so she decided to appreciate the vulnerability it represented and another set of easy to exploit traits she would use in the future.

The mission she reminded herself, *the mission*, get in, get what you want, get out, and leave the refuse behind. She sat patiently, and watched as the experienced bar manager had observed what was going on, and in true Thai spirit, insisted that he play her, a challenge he couldn't resist, and when she soundly and quickly defeated him in three consecutive games, Fern watched as he laughed with the other girls and that it didn't seem to have gotten his feathers ruffled. She made note.

A British guy sitting at the bar was lathered, and unable to keep his voice down, and after the third or fourth reminder by the staff. Chase took it as a sign that he too had let his guard down too much by drinking and spending money too freely. While the expense was inconsequential monetarily, what it displayed was not what he wanted, because he knew he was showing weakness, both in terms of self-control but also by appearing too generous, both traits he knew Thais saw as weakness, especially the girls who worked the bars.

He needed to regain control and had to change locations to do so, for he had blown up this spot, and he was no longer any good here. He didn't have time to chastise himself, he had to act and move, so he suggested they head back in the direction of his hotel. Fern just nodded, spoke a few words quietly to the girls from the bar and bowed, hands held together pointing up in front of her respectfully as they left.

Chase had noticed how deferential Fern was to the other women working in the bar. He understood how territorial these girls were of their places of employment and how competition in places like this by girls who were freelancing would not be tolerated. Because she was with him, meant that she was welcome, as long as she stayed with him, and he continued to spend money. They knew farang liked to take girls barhopping and it was both understood and accepted, but it didn't mean she could come in acting high and mighty or better than they, and she certainly was respectful, deferential, and always appropriate, easily aligning with them to drain the most out of the man she was with for their mutual benefit and Chase was no different. After all, it was just work for them, and of course, for her.

Bangla Road Goodbye

They walked back down Bangla Road together. The street pulsed with life. As they neared Soi Sea Dragon, Fern paused. She sensed that the night was coming to an end at his discretion, always "at the customer's discretion", and while he hadn't paid her bar fine or short-time rate, she nevertheless saw him as her customer, regardless of what he thought it was, and if he wanted the night to continue, wanted more of her time, or of her, that was something she had to let him raise on his own. Her job was to remain neutral, available, willing, for whatever, and then state the price if and when it came to that.

The bar lights illuminated her face just enough for him to notice how plain she looked now. Her makeup had melted away. Her hair frizzed in the humidity. Without heels, she was tiny beside him, and she looked unimpressive in her street clothes. There were at least twenty younger, prettier girls within shouting distance.

But none of them were *her*.

She looked up at him, waiting. Expecting. He looked her in the eyes, held her gaze as she smiled up at him. He wanted to take her in his arms, lift her off her feet, hug her so tightly she would moan, kiss her mouth deeply, more. But he did none of those things. He resisted the urge to go weak for her femininity, for how in her unpolished, unfiltered by the makeup and lights of the club, she looked even more desirable than before. He resisted giving up control by succumbing to the simplicity of her sexuality, to his desire and impulse, knowing that level of control in the hands of a woman who was trained, who made a living knowing how to manipulate it was peril for him in that moment. And yet, in that instant, she was the most beautiful, and the only woman on the entire Bangla Road that he saw.

"Thanks for tonight. I had a great time. You're a really cute kid". And then his go to, "See you later."

She blinked, caught off guard.

As he turned and walked away, she called after him, "Thanks."

He waved without turning back, her gaze burning into him as he disappeared toward the beach.

Chapter Four

The Edge of the Line

"All warfare is based on deception. Hence, when we are able to attack, we must seem unable; when using our forces, we must appear inactive... When near, we must make the enemy believe we are far away; when far away, we must make him believe we are near."—
Sun Tzu, The Art of War

The moment he turned and walked away, Fern stood motionless, caught in the strange electricity of a scene she hadn't expected. Her weight shifted slightly, instinctively preparing for the moment he'd pivot back, offer a smirk and a hand, deliver some excuse to pull her toward his room. The final page of the same old script she'd acted in a thousand times before.

But Chase never turned around.

He kept walking, the casual wave over his shoulder so confidently final it felt like punctuation. Not a pause—an ending. And for just a moment, she couldn't move.

She blinked, forced a small smile, and turned in the opposite direction. Her heart beat faster than she wanted, and not from excitement—but confusion. Frustration. Intrigue. She hadn't misread the signs. The way he'd leaned into her during dinner, the tightness of her arms around him on the ride, how his hand had lingered on the small of her back a beat too long at the bar. And yet... he didn't make a move. He'd let her go.

She should've been relieved. Hell, she should've been smug. It meant her instincts were right: he was playing her, trying to prove he wasn't like the others. That he respected her. That he was trustworthy. That he was trying to win her over.

But then why did it feel like she had been played?

Why was she suddenly embarrassed, glancing to see if the other girls on the street had seen the farang walk away and leave her standing there? If even one had, she would have lost face. She looked down at her feet, kept moving. She didn't look around.

It bothered her.

Not that she wanted him to fuck her—of course not, he was a sweaty farang—but the fact that he didn't try scared her. Was she losing her touch faster than she could afford? And getting him to pay her for short time would have been a nice cap to an otherwise decent evening.

But in the end, all she had was time spent—no payout, no progress. Just confusion.

Back in his room, Chase let the silence settle around him like armor.

He hadn't turned on the TV. Didn't need to. The images of the night replayed just fine without it. Fern's laugh, her hand brushing his arm when she told him about the food from her home. The way she looked with wind-blown hair, makeup melted off, stripped of all pretense. Real. Vulnerable in a way that struck him deeper than he'd expected.

And that moment, back at the bar.

The girl he'd been playing pool with was cute—playful even—and she had a body he liked. But when Fern offered her up like a drink refill, like he was just another commodity that she could trade to help a fellow Thai, it hit him harder than he expected. He played it cool. Said the right things. Held the line.

Not because he was trying to impress her. But because he had to believe he was different.

He wanted to be different, at least with her, but why?

The truth he didn't want to look at too closely—he was more like his father than he'd ever admit, cold, strategic, and emotionally compartmentalized. Always wanting to be in control, and never really caring about anyone or anything but himself. He was always safe, never in a position to be touched emotionally by anyone, invulnerable.

The distance his father had always used as a weapon and control tactic in his marriage and with the other wife and family he maintained was the same one Chase was trying to use now. Watching Fern through a one-way mirror. Letting her get close just enough to feel wanted, but not enough to threaten his center and his sense of safety.

But she was threatening it anyway and while he didn't want to admit it, the fact that he thought about her as often as he did, the fact that he was willing to expend his time, be pulled away from his purpose, to be near her, the fact that he wanted to be in her presence betrayed the illusion of control he was desperately, delusionally, trying to maintain. And what he didn't yet realize was that he was more like her in that sense than he could appreciate, for she too needed that same sense of distance and control, that same sense of emotional detachment. The inevitable question would be which one needed it more.

The Next Morning – Separate Spaces, Shared Thoughts

Chase sat at the hotel restaurant, sipping black coffee and watching the beach from the shaded veranda. The tide crawled in lazily, the morning tourists trickling out with towels and sun hats. He hadn't messaged Fern. He wanted to. But he couldn't afford to. He needed her to feel the pull. To reach out. To wonder. To want. Control was critical, and he deluded himself into thinking that he was somehow steering this shipwreck in the making, instead of being pulled under along with the rest of the wreckage.

He tried to put himself in her position, in "their" position. Coming from a Western, affluent country, and having never been brought up around real poverty, he knew it was impossible to understand what their lives or experiences were like. And Thai culture—the apparent paradoxes and intricacies of how their social structure and hierarchies blended with their primary religion—further complicated his understanding of how women who worked the bars saw and understood the world around them.

The concept of planning for one's future, he'd been told, was foreign to them—something he struggled to grasp. The way most Thais thought of money, the "live for today" mentality—made it hard for him to relate to most of the women he had encountered up to this point. Their fidelity to care for their families, the ways daughters often became the primary financial providers, was something that he could only understand abstractly as it was so far removed from how he saw or what he would ever expect from his own daughter.

In the West, sure, some men prided themselves on being pimps, but it was unheard of for a mother or father, brother, boyfriend, or husband to actually expect—or even demand—that their daughter, sister, girlfriend, or wife prostitute herself to provide a better life for the family. To be a pimp in the literal sense was to be a parasite, low-life, piece of shit, and to pander one's own loved one was incomprehensible. While it inevitably happened, it was so obscure and rare that the vast majority of Westerners never actually encountered it in real life. It existed on the lowest rung of the social ladder, invisible to the middle land even lower class of working Americans.

Chase pondered these apparent paradoxes in his mind as he contemplated his next move. He knew he had to maintain a respectful approach. To do that, he would have to temper the impact of his biases and judgments on his demeanor, speech, and mannerisms. Fern was far too observant, too shrewd, too attuned to nuance not to pick up on subtle cues. Likely far more than Chase could understand or appreciate. She would dissect his body language and parse his silences. And he wasn't sure if that made him more impressed—or more afraid.

Nok, the senior waitress, stopped to offer a refill on his coffee, and looked at him with the same bemused smile she had for him every morning. She queried, "You happy today, Kha?" Chase smiled back, he and Nok had engaged in this conversation before, and he knew what was coming next. He responded, "Happy, is that important to you Khub?" They had a way of dodging each other's questions that had, over the years that Chase had been coming to the same resort, become a bit of a game between the two of them. She: "You alone again today, Kha," which at this point had become a statement more than it was a question, as she had made it known in the past that she noticed he never brought a woman to breakfast with him. Chase merely smiled back and stated that the coffee was good today. He realized several trips back that he had become a bit of a mystery to her, and had observed how she and the other staff would watch him each morning sitting alone, staring out at the ocean through his sunglasses, while sipping his morning coffee, always alone, and for a moment he wondered what she must have thought about him.

Fern

Fern sat crossed legged in the middle of the floor of the shared room, sipping cold instant coffee from a cracked mug, while letting her hair air dry from her morning shower. She was already plotting. The emotional hook was set. That much was clear.

He respected her, and he wanted her to know that he did. That was another trait on the growing list of noticeable chinks in his armor. He was so typically Western in his understanding of the culture and the intricacies of Thai social structure that he didn't even realize how far out of his depth he really was. That made him even more vulnerable, she thought. It never registered that his respect for her could be legitimate, that what he saw in her, was her ideal self, what she was capable of being, and that he was able to look past everything else, see that potential, and desire it and *her* for it. Because she couldn't ever want or even hope for him to love her, she didn't fathom that he could or that he ever would, and she certainly didn't think for one moment that it was possible that he already did.

Not to mention, it was obvious he had the additional fatal flaw most of these men carried—the Hero Complex. For fuck's sake, they were raised on Disney movies where the woman is always helpless and in need of saving, and the man is the one with all the strength, always looking for someone to rescue so he can feel whole.

But it wasn't just that. There was also the validation these men got from thinking they could provide for or take care of a woman. Their masculinity became defined by their ability to spend, to lavish, to support. That was how so many of them felt like men—like successes. And women like Fern used that like a weapon.

It was how the bars worked. How the entire ecosystem thrived.

The women didn't sell love or often even the illusion of it. They sold affirmation. Identity. They held up mirrors and let men see what they wanted to see. And in exchange, the girls took what they needed—money, security, options. But if it was love he wanted to buy, well the illusion of that was certainly available too, but of course, the price was much higher, more so than she knew he could fathom.

She would exploit those tendencies—the insecurities, the needs, and the romantic delusions—like she had done many times before. If he wanted to play the game, fine. To the victor would go the spoils. After all, she didn't owe him anything. And if his little heart was already broken, so what, it was now about to be annihilated.

And it didn't surprise her anymore to realize he was trying to do the same thing.

She imagined him back at his hotel, maybe sipping coffee and replaying the night. Strategizing. Thinking himself clever. Believing he had some moral and intellectual edge. Some special insight because of his education and privileged background.

But none of them ever did.

They who thought they could beat the girls at Connect Four, and then when they couldn't, it was their arrogance that kept them lulled into the fatal error of thinking they could beat these girls, and this system, at their real game. Fools were the lifeblood of the industry.

And Fern? She was preparing for harvest.

Chapter Five

Saltwater and Smoke

"The greatest power of a seducer is the ability to detach. It is a psychic shield that allows you to play with danger and seduce without being seduced."—
Robert Greene, The Art of Seduction

The rain was warm and relentless by the time they finished lunch—one of those thick tropical downpours that felt personal and oddly theatrical, as if the sky itself were leaning into their moment. Chase had insisted on paying, as always, and Fern hadn't objected. There was something unspoken in their interactions now, an ease masked as casualness, but every exchange was freighted with deeper strategy, like a subtle game of chess played in slow motion. When they stepped outside and stood beneath the overhang, watching the water sheet down in glimmering veils, she didn't move.

She tilted her face upward, letting the rain soak into her hair, her thin T-shirt clinging to her body like silk, eyes closed, smiling faintly. "You ever ride in the rain?" she asked, the gleam in her eye both mischievous and strangely intimate.

"Not when I had a choice," Chase replied, his grin disarming.

They climbed onto the bike without another word, surrendering to the moment. As they weaved through the traffic on Second Road, water spraying in arcs around them, Fern's arms tightened around his waist, her cheek pressed against his back. There was something primal in the motion, the sound of tires hissing over flooded asphalt, the heavy scent of wet pavement and fish sauce lingering in the air. Chase rode with the kind of precision and restraint that spoke volumes—not performative bravado, but a quiet confidence that made Fern uneasy in the way only real control ever could. Not the grasping, desperate type the others always had. No, this was something different. And that made it more dangerous.

He had grown up around motorcycles, riding since he was a small boy on the backroads and trails in Northwestern Pennsylvania. Motorcycling was not just a hobby, but a passion of his, whether it was through the canyons of southern California, or the long stretches of open road, Chase loved it all, and found no greater sense of freedom then when he was alone on the open road on a bike. Riding was second nature to him and he loved the feel of her behind him, hurling themselves forward through space and time together, and he wondered if she could sense how perfect he felt life was in that moment, the two of them together, not needing to speak to feel connected, just themselves, the bike, and the movement.

When the wind shifted and she began to shiver, he pulled the bike into a gap between parked scooters near a row of massage shops on the quieter end of the street. Without waiting for her answer, he called over his shoulder, "Let's get massages until the rain stops."

They dismounted together, drenched and laughing, their soaked clothes slapping wetly against their bodies. As they approached a shop staffed by a group of smiling ladyboys, Fern gently nudged him aside and led him into the next storefront—a quieter place, with older women behind the counter, she would later reveal the workers here were friends of hers.

Inside, they peeled off their shoes, accepted towels, and were guided to adjacent curtained cubicles. Lying side-by-side on padded mats, the buzz of fluorescent lights above them, the rain still hammering the thin roof like a heartbeat, they let the day fold into something quiet.

"You like this?" she asked eventually, eyes half-lidded, her voice low.

"This?" he smirked. "Rain? Massage shops? Or being mostly naked in public with a woman who laughs at me?"

She smiled but didn't answer. The moment was enough.

As her massage began, she heard him explaining—in broken, charming Thai—that he didn't want his feet touched. The masseuse giggled, called him tukatee, and he laughed along, like he understood. Fern allowed herself a small smile. He was learning, but he still didn't understand the rules. Not the real ones.

They didn't speak much. Not then. But there was something in the way their glances lingered when the curtain fluttered or their hands nearly brushed across the mat that made the silence feel more danger-ous than words.

Later, after the rain had faded to a mist and the air was thick with heat and ozone, they walked along the beach barefoot. Fern's sequined skirt glinted in the fading light, strangely fitting against the shimmering, reflective sand. The tide had pulled far out, leaving pools of water and scattered shells. She walked close, occasionally reaching for his hand, but never holding it long.

He bought her a cheap, technicolor ice cream cone from a roadside cart, and she performed gratitude in exaggerated tones. "Oh, thank you, kind sir," she said with mock reverence, playing the doe-eyed ingénue. He chuckled but didn't push. That too, she noticed.

"You ever do this?" he asked, motioning toward the surf.

Fern paused, her toe tracing a line in the wet sand before stepping into the waves. "First time."

"You live here," he said, more surprised than accusatory.

She gave a slight shrug. "Working girls don't play. Not unless there's a reason."

He couldn't tell if it was a lie, or if the lie itself held a different truth. She sat beside him on the low seawall, licking at the cone with a laziness that was almost sensual. He found himself watching the melting trail as it trickled down her wrist. She let it happen. Let him see. Whether it was intentional or not, it worked. He wasn't sure if she had never eaten an ice cream cone before or if she just didn't care that her hands were getting all sticky, he didn't know what to make of it.

Back near Nanai Road, he took her to a beer bar he clearly knew. The air was heavy with fried garlic and sweat. Chase played Connect Four and pool with the bar girls, his charm subtle but consistent. He wasn't showing off. He didn't need to. Fern watched him from the corner, her glass of Chiang sweating in her hand. She played a few rounds, let him win twice, beat him once.

Inside, her thoughts were louder than the chatter around her. She knew the window was closing. If he didn't make a move tonight, she would lose the initiative—and more worryingly, lose the narrative. Another, darker part of herself wanted him to take her back to his room and use her sexually, objectify her, treat her like a toy for his pleasure, even hurt her if he wanted to. The darkness of her thoughts was not foreign to her; these types of thoughts and feelings came up from time to time. When and why they came up was mostly unpredictable, and while she thought she knew their origin, she never let herself ponder the source too long.

Was she trying to replicate something from her past to feel in control? Was she wanting to validate some deeply held belief that she had about herself, how men saw her, what she felt she deserved or was worth. She didn't know. She just knew she wanted him to use her. If that happened, she would know once and for all exactly where she stood with him, and she would feel in control, her beliefs validated, and not at all confused. She didn't like feeling confused.

Across the bar, Chase wrestled with something far less defined. The moment was there. It was approaching. The unspoken beat in the seduction rhythm, the place where most men reached for the final move. But he didn't want her like that. Or rather, he didn't want her just like that.

He had made the mistake he swore not to make. He respected her. And that respect had started to tangle with something closer to affection. Worse—he liked who she was. Not what she did. Not just how she looked. Who she was. Or who he thought she might be beneath all of this. It was her intelligence, her obvious determination, and her ability to be whatever the situation demanded, that he found alluring.

She was interesting, and he realized, that for the longest time, he had not felt that towards any of the women in his life, not really, and if so, not for very long. He always knew exactly where he stood with them and rarely if ever really cared one way or the other. He was always detached, liked being so, felt comfortable there, but now was different. She was different, regardless of if he wanted her to be or not.

He knew what that meant. And he knew the cost.

And it was that word, *cost*, that was at the heart of why he didn't ask her to come back to his room for an hour or so before her shift started. Because he wasn't sure he was ready if she said yes and then set a price. Not that the money would matter, no matter how ridiculous the short time rate she may quote. It was the idea that if she set a price, he would know he would never be anything more than a customer to her and it was that truth he wasn't ready to face. So, he avoided the situation where it would come up, because he wasn't ready to accept that she could never see him as anything more than a customer. That was the moment, he would realize much later, that he knew he was totally fucked.

They walked back to Bangla Road just before sunset, the sky above them lit in streaks of blood and gold. Just before the edge of walking street, she stopped.

"This is where we say goodbye for now," she said.

"I'll see you tonight," he replied. "It's my last night in town and I want to watch you dance."

"Ok Kha, I'll see you later tonight then."

"I'll stop by. Sit for a bit. Maybe buy you a drink or two."

She didn't answer, just turned and walked ahead. He stayed back, deliberately creating distance.

He easily respected her boundaries, never pushed up against them out of neediness or a clingy desire to remain close to her. She set a limit and he accepted it without hesitation, or push-back. She hated how much that made her respect him, and she should have made note of what it could mean in the future, but for once she didn't think it that far ahead, because she had allowed herself to feel the warmth of their time together, had let her guard down just enough to consider "*what if*" not what's next.

Later That Night – The Room, The Mirror, and the Rift

Back in the room she shared with Fon and the other girls, Fern sat in front of the mirror, applying her makeup with slow, robotic precision. Around her, the other girls gossiped and traded stories like poker chips. Fon laid on the bed, watching her.

"You're different lately," Fon said finally, voice flat.

Fern didn't respond.

"You're thinking about him again. The American."

"He's just another customer."

Fon snorted. "He hasn't paid you once."

Fern tightened her grip on the eyeliner. "He will. Or he won't. Doesn't matter."

"You think he's going to save you?" Fon sat up now, her tone sharper. "You think he's going to take you away? Buy you a house in the hills and let you quit all this?"

Fern turned slowly, locking eyes with her. "And if I did?"

Fon stood and crossed the room. "Then you're a fool. Just like the others."

"I'm not like them."

"No," Fon said, her voice low and venomous. "You're worse. Because you think you're different."

Their stares clashed like blades in silence. Fern knew Fon had already gone to the handlers. She could smell it—see it in the way Fon's eyes flinched, the way her mouth twitched like she wanted to say more but didn't.

Fon wasn't just hurt. She was dangerous now. She was spiraling. Because Chase wasn't just another trick. He represented something else—power. An option. Escape. And if Fern took that option if it actually presented itself, Fon would lose everything and be left alone without her. She realized, Fon could never be happy for her, glad she had gotten lucky, but she quickly reminded herself, she hadn't gotten anything yet, and the thought pulled her back to the reality of what her life really was, all built off illusion. It was something that she had come to at least think she understood and something she had thought she had learned to work with, effectively leveraging it to stay in control.

"Stay away from him," Fon whispered. "Or I swear I'll ruin it. You don't get to walk out. Not unless they let you. Not unless I do too!"

Fern didn't answer. But in her chest, something dark and hot burned.

And still, doubt crept in. She hated feeling torn between hoping and being in control. To her hope was such a helpless feeling, something she hated, and had spent years of her life avoiding. Replacing it with whatever she had to tell herself to *feel* in control, as that was the only place she ever truly felt safe.

As she sat alone later, legs tucked beneath her, letting her hair dry naturally before getting dressed for the evening, she stared out at the blinking neon bleeding through the curtain. Would he even show up tonight? Would he really return to the club, buy her drinks, talk to her like none of the pressure existed? Maybe he was bluffing. Maybe he had already decided to cut bait, disappear into the haze of another flight, another life. Why did she even think he wasn't "playing" with other girls in the other clubs. Had she assumed that he wasn't pulling this shit with at least a few other girls in town. After all, she was just one of thousands. Doubt was deadly. She hated it as much as she hated hope, and now she felt like she was being pulled apart in opposite directions by the two. It was agonizing and she wondered how she had ever let herself get to this point.

In that moment, she pulled back to put things in perspective, like Chase himself had done, and she told herself that the truth was every night he walked to her club to come see her he had to walk by at least a hundred or more girls, younger and prettier than her, most either calling out to him or literally tugging on his arm to get his attention. That at any time, he could go into any of those massage shops, bars or clubs, or pick up a freelancer on the street or from one of the numerous "dating" apps and have them in his room within minutes. That was the reality. So why then did he always come back to *her* club for *her*, never expressing the slightest interest in any of the other girls. She wrestled with the dissonant thoughts. Why hadn't he just fucked her already? Why was he being so patient?

She had seen it before—men make promises in the afternoon and disappear by nightfall.

But she sensed that Chase was different. And that made her doubt everything more.

If he shows up, she told herself, tonight is the night. She would have to make her move, seal the illusion, close the circuit. If she didn't, if she let the last night pass without anchoring him—physically, emotionally—she risked losing him forever, and she wasn't going to do that, not without something of monetary value in return. She resigned herself to keep him as a mark, and in that moment, she felt better, *hope*, at least for now vanquished, and replaced with control, and she felt safe again.

And yet, she hated how badly she wanted him to come back. Not just because she needed to win. But because somewhere beneath the game, she needed to feel chosen.

At the Hotel

Chase sat on the edge of his bed, suitcase half-zipped, staring at nothing.

The lines had blurred. Whatever this started as, it wasn't that anymore. He reminded himself that Fern was playing him. That this was all strategy. But he still hadn't been played like this. Not in years. Maybe not ever. Yuyi, his girl in Chengdu, had run game on him years back—a different play, but unmistakable in its intent.

She had tested him hard one night when they were in Tokyo together about four years ago. They'd spent the day shopping, laughing, drinking too much Sapporo in a Shibuya alley bar, and somewhere between the seventh beer and the slow walk back to the hotel, she pushed his buttons. Kept bringing up exes, imaginary admirers, seeing how far she could needle him. He'd tried to keep his cool at first, but when she smirked and said maybe she'd just head off with someone else, he lost it. Told her to carry her own shit, shoved the bags of things he'd bought into her hands, and stormed off alone. Half a block later, he realized she wasn't behind him. She wasn't answering texts. He knew she was playing a game, should have been prepared and not bothered by it, but he was annoyed. He went back to their room and passed out. When he woke up around midnight, there she was—sitting cross-legged in the corner of the room, crying quietly, as if the act itself had earned her the right to be hurt. That was manipulation with makeup smeared under her eyes.

But Fern? Fern was another level entirely. She never raised her voice. Never flinched. Never even asked for anything. That was what made her dangerous. She was running a game, but she didn't need to push. She let you walk into the trap yourself.

She hadn't made the ask yet. But when she did, he'd have to make the only move that still gave him power. He whispered it to himself like a line from a play:

"I can never be your customer. If this is going to mean anything when I move here in three years, that can never be part of the story."

But now, the whisper felt hollow, because he knew how stupid it sounded.

Because this wasn't just about power anymore. It had started as a test. Just a seduction puzzle—could he make her fall for him? Could he draw her out, play her like she had played so many others? He wanted to see if he could get the ultimate cool girl to let down her guard.

He never imagined he'd get caught in the web himself.

Fern had become something more. She had stopped being a game and started being the game board—the whole thing. He hated how much he admired her composure, her resolve, her intelligence. He hated how much he wanted her to want him, not because of what he had, but because of who he was. And most of all, he hated that despite everything he knew, everything he had studied, everything he had practiced, he was unsure of what she'd do next—or what he would do if she finally asked.

He hoped it would be enough. He feared it was already too late.

Chapter Six

The Last Night

THE CLUB WAS ALREADY buzzing by the time Fern stepped onto the stage for her first set. The lighting was just dim enough to hide flaws and just bright enough to turn sequins into seduction. She moved like clockwork—slow, sensual, economical in energy—but her eyes kept darting to the entrance, waiting.

Chase didn't show until well after midnight, later than usual, and when he did, Fern noticed it instantly—not just the lateness, but the scent that clung to his shirt. Underneath the familiar smell she had come to unconsciously associate with safety and stimulation was a distinct, floral trace of perfume. It wasn't hers but was a typical scent used by other working girls.

She tried not to react but caught herself adjusting her posture, smoothing a line that didn't need fixing. Was he playing her? Had he found someone else to toy with before showing up? Or was he making a point? A test? Her mind churned even as her body kept up the motions.

He had come to Bangla Road early that night, determined to stall his arrival at her club. He wasn't ready to end things. Not yet. Not while the streets pulsed with that uniquely Phuket mix of neon, sweat, and invitation. Walking Street was alive in that specific way it always was near the end of high season—girls calling out in half-broken English, DJs remixing early 2000's pop hits, tourists stumbling in packs of three and four, beer towers on their tables and laughter a little too loud. Touts and girls alike, three or four at time, clutching at your arm as you walked by, trying to hustle you into their establishment or to buy them a drink or freelancers hustling for short time dates. Chase had gotten good at dodging them as he walked deliberately towards his favorite Go-Go in the far-right corner of the Soi. This was where he preferred to begin each night. As he entered, Rob Zombie's "Never Gonna Stop Me" was pumping through the PA system as five dancers, three completely nude, gyrated on the stage in the center of the small club.

As soon as he sat down, a dancer, maybe twenty-one, walked up and sat next to him brushing her hand deliberately across his thigh and groping for his tool, leaning in close and whispered about what she could do behind the curtain as she nodded towards the back of the room. Her skin smelled of coconut and body spray. Her body too perfect to ignore. The desperation for a customer thinly vailed. He got hard. She noticed. Smiled. Pulled his hand toward her and rubbed it between her legs. "VIP?" she leaned into him, lips brushing his ear as she offered in a practiced murmur. "Anything you want."

For a flicker of a second, he hesitated. The temptation was real. Mechanical. Easy. But something in him recoiled. He pulled his hand away gently, stood, gave her a polite nod, and walked back out into the street.

He hated how he felt after. Weak. Predictable. But somehow—stronger for walking away. The truth was, the cheap and easy sex was never really his thing. He never had a problem getting pussy at home, and rarely got turned on by strangers, no matter how hot they were physically, coming onto him in obviously fake and contrived ways. In short, feeling like a sucker created too much cognitive dissonance for him to get into it. He knew he spent too much time in his own head, but he couldn't help it. It was who he was. For him to be truly turned on required something else, a sense that he was in control and that the attraction was mutual even if at times there was a transactional nature behind the exchange. He realized that was Fern's strength, at least one of them with him anyway. She was either just that good at convincing him that she wanted him too or, perhaps maybe, the thinnest of chances that she actually did.

His mind flashed back to the last time he was in Phuket about a year ago, how a freelancer with her belongings in a plastic shopping bag and wearing yoga shorts kept following him asking if he wanted a date when he had turned off of Bangla Road and had headed back to his hotel. He said no, but couldn't help but do a double take, as girls in yoga shorts was a personal weakness, and how as she kept following him, almost begging, and how as he continued to refuse, but look, she continued to follow.

It had aroused him in a way he didn't understand. It turned quickly into a game, he'd say no, but look back at her, and she would continue to follow. The game continued all the way to the door of his hotel and by that time he was rock hard and knew he was going to fuck her. He was actually grateful that he had gotten that aroused and when he let her slip into his room behind him, he was glad he had.

Ok, so he knew he had issues, and fucking freelancers was about as dumb as you could get, he knew all of that, but what he was up to on this trip was taking stupid to a whole other level. Now was his chance to choose smart, but of course, he didn't.

By the time he stepped into Fern's club, he'd gathered himself. But the perfume from the girl in the previous bar had lingered on his shirt, and he hadn't noticed. Fon caught it first, not Fern.

She walked past Chase's table slowly, then circled back with her trademark grin and as she sat down uninvited and slid up next to him, far too close for his comfort—a curl of the mouth that always hinted at venom. "You smell different tonight," she said in English, loud enough for Fern to hear as she was sitting down on his other side. "Something sweet. Not like beer. Or your usual," she kept pushing.

Chase smiled. "Okay, and your breath smells like mouth wash, busy night huh?" he stated, trying to appear indifferent and brushing it off, while making a not-so-subtle dig.

Fon leaned in even closer almost whispering in his ear, "You didn't come last night. That was Fern's night off." Her voice was bright. But the look she gave him was surgical. "People around here notice things like that you know," she hissed in a much less playful and much more ominous tone as she stood and walked away leaving the two of them alone on the couch in the center of the club.

Still, when Chase turned to put his arm around Fern, she noticed everything. His warmth, the feel of his arm around her should and the soft and delicate yet deliberate way his hand caressed her arm as he whispered "I missed you" into her ear, and the perfume.

They talked, laughed a little, but even that had edges. When the music dipped and things grew quiet, he turned toward her, voice low. "I leave tomorrow," he said. "Flying to Chengdu for a week. Then home."

She nodded, the look on her face giving nothing away. "I hope we can stay in touch while I'm gone. I'll be back in six months. This time for a full month. Maybe we can spend some real time together. Alone." She smiled, but it didn't reach her eyes, those remained cold, distant, but calculating.

Then came the moment she expected—and didn't. "I never bar-fined you," he said. "And I never will. If we're going to have any future... that can't be part of it."

She blinked. Smiled again. Tilted her head like the words were sweet, and the innocent girl in her was hearing them and that they mattered, that they were touching to her, that she thought they were sincere. All of that, the perfect reaction, instinctual, professional, and automatic. She was that good, and she reminded herself to stay focused and in frame, now was the moment to seal things for later, a later that would unfold over time, three years to be precise, but this was pivotal, and she knew that intuitively.

But inside? She almost laughed. He didn't get it. He couldn't. There were roles in this world—seducer and seduced, buyer and seller. And he was still clinging to the illusion that he could stand outside the rules just by declaring them. Still, he intrigued her. Not because of his refusal, but because of the foolish sincerity behind it. He still believed in fairy tales. That added to his vulnerability. And the fact that he was working this hard for something meant he was invested and wouldn't walk away easily. That was currency. It had value and she wasn't going to let him go unpunished for it.

And yet, when she returned from her final set, she slid into the couch beside him, straddled his lap like she'd done before. This time, the kissing was different—messier, urgent, less for show. When his hand slipped beneath her bikini bottom, she didn't stop him. When his fingers found her clit, she spread her legs a little. Let him touch her. Let herself feel it.

Her body responded before she gave permission.

Later, in the dressing room, she thought about the small, dark stain she had left that marked the front of his pants. He'd left with it still wet. Was it strategy? Instinct? Had she even wanted him?

She didn't know. "Of course not," she told herself, and didn't have to remind herself how she hated most of these men almost instinctively. So why had she felt something?" Men touched her intimately every night, and if they bought her drinks, she gave them lap dances, rubbed their cocks through their pants, and if they took her to the VIP section in the back of the club, even more, and if they bar fined her, they got whatever they wanted. He was nothing special, so what he touched her there, lots of guys do most nights, it's just part of the job, she thought.

Why then did his touch feel different? Sure, it was not rough, crude, and it didn't feel dirty. It felt like he was making love to her with his hand, at least in his mind. "Stupid" she told herself, "Stop being stupid". He was a pig like the rest of them, perhaps just a bit more polished, but a pig nonetheless.

He waited for her this time—not while she was on stage, but while she was beside him again. Before he stood to leave, he said that he wasn't one for long goodbyes, and something along the lines of him "seeing her in six months", and then he stood and walked away. As she stood, her lips parted as if she might say something and he caught a glimpse as she turned sharply and walked quickly towards the dressing room and disappeared behind the velvet curtain, that her eyes stung and that they may have been on the verge of tears. She didn't want him to see, but he did, and he wasn't sure if she was truly emotional, or if it was all part of her ploy and completely performative. He chose the latter.

The next morning, she texted him and offered to take him to the airport. He wrote back fast, saying "a friend with a car had already offered," and that he had accepted her invitation.

"No problem," she typed.

She then sat in silence. That was a problem. She hated that it wasn't her. It wasn't so much that someone else got that final moment, she told herself. She didn't care about the sentimentality, instead, she wouldn't have the opportunity to show a greater investment, something that he would value. Also, was there a "her", someone else angling for him, competition for her, or more likely, was he just working an angle to make her feel jealous. She didn't know for sure. The way he declined her offer so casually—it cut, and it was surprising. That was one thing about

Chase, as predictable as he could be at times, there were others when he didn't respond in the textbook "Dumb Farang" way. That both bothered and made her have to think more than usual.

She knew Chengdu well. Had worked there. What kind of work, he never asked. He never asked much, actually—not about the club, not about the men that she entertained, not about the past. That used to be a relief. Now, it felt like disinterest.

She looked at her reflection in the window of the coffee shop near her apartment. The makeup she hadn't washed off the night before was still there in smudged lines. She looked tired. Older.

Fon had noticed everything. The perfume. The wet patch. The way the manager had been watching. And Fon had already made her move. Gone to the handlers. Reinforced her position.

There would be consequences. Expectations. They always followed attention. And the attention now wasn't just on Fern. It was on him. She had told herself this was strategy. That he was a mark. That the power was hers.

As she watched him walk away through the club's neon flicker in her memory, she felt the silence in her life settle like smoke.

She began to wonder if she had become the mark.

Act Two

Chapter Seven

Shadows on the Line

CHASE SIPPED HIS WHISKEY slowly in the lounge of Phuket International Airport, watching planes taxi across the rain-dappled runway. A low hum of conversation and soft jazz filtered through the room, but it was the vibration of his phone that commanded his attention. A message from Fern. Another one. Short. Sweet. "Miss you already, my superman."

He read it twice. Then a third time. The "my superman"—was a private joke between them. One of those nicknames that creeps in through the back door of affection, subtle and oddly powerful. He typed back, then erased. Typed again. Erased. In the end, he simply wrote: "Thinking of you too. Stay safe tonight," then reminded her "I'm just an ordinary guy, no superman."

His flight to Chengdu would take five hours. Five hours to think. To reflect. To recalibrate. But even as he boarded the plane, reclined in his pod seat, and let the hush of international air travel embrace him, Fern was still in his head.

And that bothered him.

He had entered this with a plan. Get in. Get access and get close. See if he could seduce her, make her love him, but keep his edge. And now, somewhere in the tangle of their time together, like the subtle but deliberate moves being made by each side in a covert war, the battle line had blurred.

Chengdu was supposed to bring clarity and reconnection to a love that had simmered on a back burner in Chase's life for the past four years. But now, it was starting to seem like it was a distraction from something he hadn't even anticipated a few short weeks prior when he had boarded the plane at LAX to start his month-long vacation in the Philippines, Thailand, and China.

Yuyi was waiting at the arrivals gate. Flowing dress, and long, jet black hair down almost to her waist. She hadn't spotted him as she paced anxiously walking between exit gates 4 and 5, which gave him the opportunity to walk up quickly behind her. As he approached, and just off her right shoulder, he whispered "excuse me, but I think we may know one another." The way she spun and jumped into his arms reminded him of the kind of love he used to believe in. When their lips met, it was heat and homecoming, her tears smeared on his cheeks as they ran down hers and she squeezed him harder than he had expected.

She hadn't changed at all in the last four years since their abrupt split in Tokyo just prior to the world's pandemic denying them physical contact and forcing them to rely on the ebb and flow of tension to maintain and deepen their connection. She was still the most beautiful woman he had ever seen, and in a place like Chengdu, that was saying something. Tears almost welled up as he felt the wave of relief wash over him, they were together again, he had pulled it off, four years of putting forth every effort he could muster to keep himself relevant in her mind and digging himself as deep as possible into her heart, and she, swaying in the same seductive dance, here they were, back in each other's arms, it seemed like a miracle, but it was true.

They didn't leave each other's side for the next ten days. The Shangri-La Hotel suite smelled of her perfume, of oolong tea, and Sichuan spice and of sex. They ran through People's Park like teenagers, visited her favorite hidden teahouses, and made love as if they were the only two people on the planet left to carry on the species. On the sixth night, she laid out a traditional tea service in his room. He cradled her in his arms as she cried quietly as they took in the floor to ceiling view of the river below as the city at night unfolded in front of them. He had promised once that he would always return for her. And for a long time, he thought she had been The One.

When the pandemic hit and locked the world down, denying them regular physical access to one another, he regretting not proposing and marrying her as she had begged him to do, choosing in his mind to never let himself get boxed in, never give up what he valued most, freedom, yet the thought of never seeing her again almost suffocated him. The weight of the missed opportunity almost crushed him, but instead, it strengthened him in ways only suffering could.

Yuyi was that special, that beautiful, that extremely rare combination of perfectly sexy, and perfectly feminine. She knew how to balance her sex appeal and beauty with the traditional Chinese female role, and she had more game than any other woman Chase had ever met, a true master of the Art of Seduction, and he simply did not want to ever live without her.

Yuyi had her own thoughts, though they rarely left her lips. She was trained—whether officially years ago, by her government handlers, or simply by life and her own survival instincts—to never let on how much she watched, and remembered, and cataloged. Chase was her favorite mark, but he wasn't just that anymore. The way he still looked at her, with reverence, with longing—it awakened her softer instincts. But also, her suspicion.

There was another woman, she could feel it in his distracted glances, the way his phone never strayed far from reach, the way his body was present but his spirit occasionally dimmed. Yuyi knew when a man was on the edge of being captured by another orbit. And she hated that she might be losing him—not to another woman necessarily—but to an idea. An illusion. That was more dangerous. She knew an independent man like Chase kept women in his life, for function, he was a man after all, and that never bothered her, but one that mattered to him was different, it was a threat, because she had plans for him, long-term plans for a future together, and she did not want that jeopardized.

She turned up her seduction slowly, expertly. The tears were real, but they were also deployed. The home-cooked meals, the silk sheets, the scent of her favorite jasmine oil rubbed on his back after sex—it was choreography. But somewhere, deeply buried beneath the games and tactics, was a strange kind of real love. She had fought hard for him. She had waited. She had believed. And now, she feared she might have been too late. He was cooler than before, not as drawn in by her subtle charms like he was years ago. He had leveled up emotionally, and in other ways, and was stronger now than when she knew him before. More evolved as a man, and that had a powerful effect on her. The truth was, she wasn't used to men like this in her life.

As a man, Chase was different, especially when compared to the average man in China she would regularly toy with or exploit. Most of them were so wedded to their mother's tit that they couldn't see past their own noses, and none certainly ever saw her the way he did, past her outward physical beauty, and to what her inner strengths and attributes were, but he did so, and at times with a razor sharpness that had left her stunned and breathless.

Additionally, he wasn't nearly as easily moved off of his emotional center, and quickly manipulated like all of the others, he was certainly unique in that way, and she found it made her love him because she respected that he saw through at least a lot of who she was, and she knew he desired and appreciated those things about her that the others were too obtuse or self-absorbed to see or appreciate.

In those ways, he too tested her, kept her sharp, and most importantly, he could make her laugh. Not the superficial silliness she would project to keep the men in her life strung along, but really laugh, from her center, and from her heart. He had that ability, to be boyish, silly, and heartfelt all at once, that she found she couldn't live without.

But now, every time Fern's name appeared on his screen, something shifted. A weight. A question. A complication. He started to realize what he had refused to name. He was falling. Not for Fern, per se. But for what Fern represented. A story. An experience. A mirror. And that—he knew—was the most dangerous kind of affection. She also, in his warped mind, gave him outs, the elusive freedom he coveted most of all. A freedom, up to know he had considered only sharing with Yuyi, now he wasn't so sure.

Fern, meanwhile, was keeping her rhythm. Late-night work. Late-night texts. Occasional selfies with ears filtered in pink or hearts hovering over her head, or more commonly, a few quick simple photos of her having dinner at a street stall with one or more of her coworkers who hadn't been long-time bar fined, often just her and Fon. Chase replied dutifully. Often quickly. Too quickly. He shared thoughts he should have filtered. Desires he should have kept to himself. He was giving her power, and he knew it.

He found himself surprised when she sent a selfie of her walking the beach in Patong, clearly the same stretch they had walked together, a picture of herself and words "I Miss You Chase and a large Heart" scrawled in the sand as the waves licked over them, her smiling in the foreground. It was a nice touch, showed planning, intent, thoughtfulness, but could he trust the authenticity of the sentiment? His rational brain screamed "hell no" but something inside him wanted to feel touched by the gesture.

He knew the rules of attraction and thought he understood female psychology. He reminded himself over and over that the game doesn't stop being played even if you want to stop playing. That there were no rests or time outs on this playing field. He would repeatedly tell himself "Don't chase. Don't overshare. Don't respond emotionally. Maintain mystery." But Fern would send a photo—slightly blurry, with a caption like "Look who misses you" or "This smile is for you" and he'd go weak, throw caution to the wind, pour out affection, respect, admiration, talk about a trait of hers he noticed and loved, something deeper about her than surface appearance.

He wanted her to know he saw her, her potential, her inner strength, and he wanted her to feel seen for those things about her he adored, but he knew he was giving her too much, and that by all the rules he had come to understand, he was ruining it for himself, that the more he revealed about how he felt, the less she would be attracted to him. Still, in his warped reasoning, he thought a woman like Fern, doing what she does for a living, may somehow respond in the opposite, and actually appreciate this kind of attention. While he knew he was wrong intellectually, he made the fatal mistake of letting his feelings move his behavior, not his logic. Women are emotional, not logical, they want to feel, not think or know what you think, he reminded himself, until they are being cunning of course.

She hadn't expected the weight of the goodbye to hit her so quickly. The first two nights after Chase's departure, she worked her shifts on autopilot, smiling at customers, dancing through sets, laughing at all the right moments. But her heart wasn't in it. When she climbed into bed those mornings, well after the sun had risen and the club's pulse had died down, it wasn't sleep that she longed for—it was silence. Stillness. Some space from the strange noise inside her chest.

She hated that she missed him. Hated the way she'd catch herself checking her phone during her breaks to see if he'd messaged. And when he did, it made her stomach twist. Not because she didn't want to hear from him. But because she did. Too much.

She had started the game. She knew that. Had played it with discipline and precision. But now the control was slipping, and she didn't understand why. Maybe it was the way he looked at her without judgment. Or how he didn't flinch when she tested him. Or how he seemed to see something in her that even she had stopped recognizing. And when she compared him to all the other men that had come through her life, he stacked up on a different level. It was not that he was better than all of them, some yes, others in some ways no, but it was the presence that he brought to her life that none of the others ever had that she found herself truly being drawn to. The consistency with which he showed up, and not out of neediness, but from some core of strength she couldn't fully grasp.

Fon noticed. Of course she did. She always did. And when Fern grew quiet between sets, or when she refused to entertain a customer's touchy flirtation with her usual poise, Fon said nothing—at first. But the side-eyes were sharper. The comments, colder. There was a shift in the air, and Fern could feel it deep within.

She replayed their last night together like a film reel burned into her mind. The way he touched her—not like a customer, not like a man buying time—but like someone who didn't just want her body, she knew he wanted her presence. She hated how much she'd wanted to stay with him that night, how close she came to asking if they could just go to his room and forget the world for a while.

But she hadn't. Because she knew what that would mean. And she wasn't sure she could handle it if he said yes. She wasn't sure if she was ready for a man to truly make love to her. The fucking she had learned to adjust to, zone out, or imagine she was in control, steering the interaction, always in character, playing a role. But feeling something warm and touching during the exchange was something she wasn't sure she was prepared for. She didn't know how she would handle giving herself emotionally over to a man or how it would feel, and it scared her.

Back in her tiny room, lying in the heat with the whir of the fan brushing her skin, she stared at the cracked ceiling and wondered if she'd already let him too far in. Her thoughts and feelings vacillated quickly between irrational idealism and a harder truth, forged in years of a reality that was constructed on illusion and carefully employed deception. And, what she was coming to realize slowly, the paradoxical draw towards an authentic love, and fear of that type of closeness. The false sense that total detachment meant strength, and that loneliness was the only alternative she could truly trust for a sense of safety.

She checked her phone again. He had replied. She smiled, and told herself it meant nothing.

She quickly wrote back anyway. She had another test in mind, at least she could continue employing them, from the long laundry list she had up her sleeve, and under that guise, could keep the dialogue, the connection going. Was she being honest with herself, or was she letting herself get swept up, did she even care anymore?

She could continue to run him through this gauntlet, seeing what he could tolerate, keeping him close, and her in control, while denying to herself that he mattered, that she cared about what they could build, and masking her fear that the floor could fall from under her at any minute.

He wasn't just losing frame. He was handing her the camera he thought. Then came the messages that made him pause.

"I think I have Dementia. Or early memory problems. My head feels... strange."

It came out of nowhere, mid-afternoon, between texts about dinner and a meme she sent of a cat passed out from drinking. He reread the sentence five times. Was it bait? A test? A genuine cry for help?

He responded by recommending that she watch the movie The Notebook.

"It's about memory, and loss, and enduring love," he typed. " It's one of my favorites and you're going to love it." The next day, before getting ready for her shift, she responded with:

"Will you be my Noah?" she asked. "I cried like a baby at the end" she went on.

His answer was measured, clinical, and he avoided the request for a romantic response. He just asked a few simple questions to assess her experience, all in rapid-fire motion: Are you struggling to stay focused and concentrate more than usual, easy to anger or get frustrated? Do you find you forget where you leave things like your keys only to find them in unusual places, have you gotten lost recently in an area you thought you knew well? and the last, and most important one, how much and how often are you drinking?

When she simply responded "yes", he didn't take the bait, at thirty-two, early onset of Cognitive Decline was highly unlikely, what was more likely was that she was drinking too much and not giving herself time to recover between episodes of regular and heavy consumption. It was a pitfall of her profession, he knew. Or just as likely, she was running a sympathy test to see if he would get overly emotionally involved.

That machine relied on alcohol to keep the girls numb and she was no different he suspected. He would get much more evidence of just how destructive a role alcohol would play in her day-to-day life as the weeks unfolded. For now, he softly suggested that she was working too hard and that she should stop drinking for thirty days and see how she feels. She changed the subject, and never brought up her fears of Dementia again, but would often let him know how significant and destructive an influence alcohol was having in her life.

He realized later that while it was true, she drank daily, a hazard of the job, it also instilled a sense of fear in the men who were interested in her and helped to fuel their rescue fantasies. She knew it supported her view in their eyes of her as a tragic figure who they could save, even if the tragic part was actually true, in her romanticized image of her life, it was nothing more than an occupational necessity.

The reality was far darker, for not just was she the embodiment of the *Puella Eterna*, she was also an alcoholic. Probably not yet completely physiologically Dependent, but almost certainly psychologically so, and certainly displaying a regular pattern of heavy overuse that was simply too true to be ignored. The lifestyle she thought was rooted in staunch independence, was appearing to Chase to be more and more just a self-destructive, soul murdering meat grinder masked as a way to make a fast fortune while maintaining a party lifestyle. He tried not to pity her, knowing it would do neither of them any good, but he couldn't help feeling that her life was just another example of wasted talent.

And then came the first of three events, the validity of which he always suspected, sensing that while at least two of them were legitimate experiences common in the lives of women like her, they were nevertheless being reported to gauge his reactions, thoughts, and outlook, more than to relate and share experiences to strengthen their connection. The first involved money and the betrayal of trust.

She told him of her roommate who stole 8,000 baht. Fern claimed it like a throwaway line—"I never trusted her anyway, then she leave, and go back to her village." But Chase suspected the story had layers. Was it a test of his protective instincts? A probe into whether he'd offer money? Or was she gauging how he would handle being betrayed, cheated, robbed. Was he prone to respond with violence, or would he be passive, shrewd, chalk it up to a loss but a valuable lesson of who could or could not be trusted? He wasn't sure.

She found his response interesting. All he said was, "hmm...seems her greed is greater than her fear, of you." He didn't offer advice about going to the police, or the manager, he didn't suggest she become aggressive or retaliatory, instead he observed the emotional dynamic and where he thought she may lie in the hierarchy within the world she lived. That interested her, as most of the guys she had run this on in the past immediately offer to "save the day" and simply send her the stolen money so she would not be out the income. But he didn't, and that made him different. He didn't take the bait, and as much as she knew he was operating from a need to rescue, his situational awareness, and ability to retain control at times was attractive.

Then her response: "Okay. I understand. You are wise." He didn't believe her, didn't think she thought he was wise, instead, he understood she was recalibrating, taking note, considering her next volley of attack, being patient, strategic, continuing to test for weakness, probe and plan.

And yet, he still saved every message. Even the ones that scared him. Even the ones that made him feel like a mark, like he knew he was getting played. Because some part of him—the part he couldn't kill, no matter how many books he read, how many rules he memorized, how many scars he wore—still believed.

Still wanted.

Still hoped.

Even if it was all smoke.

Even if the real fire hadn't started yet.

Chapter Eight

The Architecture of Absence

BACK IN CALIFORNIA, CHASE stepped out of the terminal into the chill of a coastal fog and a world that suddenly felt too clean, too quiet, too antiseptic. The city moved around him in efficient rhythms—polished cars on six-lane highways, earbuds, protein shakes, scheduled lives. His own home felt foreign. Spartan. His furniture austere. The mattress too firm. The air too sterile. And still, somehow, everything reminded him faintly of Fern. Of tequila and lime-flavored kisses, stripper sweat, and intrigue.

His nights filled quickly with work—his clinical practice was flourishing and his investments growing steadily. During the day he slept, worked out, read, cooked his own meals, and put in his eight hours working mostly from home at his job with the government, as a civil servant, he had learned to do the minimum required, nothing more and because of his own puritanical work ethic, nothing less. On paper, he was the same man, but inside, something shifted. Something jagged. Something focused and sharp.

Fern kept texting. Sometimes just emojis. Sometimes blurry photos of her food or feet or the view of Bangla Road at 4 or 5 am. Sometimes she wrote paragraphs, other times, single lines. Often sweet. Sometimes sad. Occasionally seductive. "Do you think of me when you wake up?" or "I dream of us every night." Most nights, she texted when her shift ended. If he didn't hear from her, he assumed she had been bar-fined, long time, and he never asked for details when she would explain the next day that she had to work late, he knew what that meant.

What unnerved him most was how natural it felt to answer. How fast his fingers moved. How easily he shared thoughts he might otherwise keep to himself, and how he had grown to look forward to her messages, checking the clock to see if she should be off work and her messages due.

They had never called each other. Not once. No late-night video chats. No voice notes. Not even a proper phone call. He had accidentally dialed her once and she messaged back instantly: "Can't talk now. Roommates asleep."

It was plausible. But also, a little too convenient. He let it go. He knew what she did, what she was, and knew that not only did he have no right to question her, no stake on her time or behavior, that doing so was weak, that jealousy was unattractive, and a feeling he must master his response to, if he ever thought they could have a real future together.

There was a rhythm to it now. She texted him before work sometimes, catching him at his most unguarded, when he would wake up in the middle of the night from an unpleasant dream or to piss. He had grown to expect it, even need it. Her messages became part of his mornings, like the hiss of the espresso machine and the hum of the fridge. He found himself responding faster, typing more. Telling her about his insomnia, his plans for the future, his ideas for how they could share a life together. She told him that he had made her change her thoughts about people and letting someone "in" despite the work she did.

He should have known better, told himself she was hustling him, but wanted to believe at least, that she wanted to believe it too, even if it only had a snow ball's chance in Hell of being real.

He had learned the term "Kay Fabe" which referred to the concept from the Professional Wrestling world, where everything was scripted and the outcomes, winners and losers, predetermined, and that it was known but the rule was that it was never overtly spoken of amongst the contestants and folks on the periphery; a created, shared illusion, that was never to be openly and intentionally discussed in public. That's what he knew they were building, and for some reason, he told himself he was okay with it.

They talked about their relationship with sleep, or at least he did. Telling her that since childhood, as early as he could remember, he would get almost completely asleep, then wake suddenly, with nothing more than a rapid heartbeat, short of breath, and a profound sense of what he could only describe as dread radiating out of the center of his chest.

He told her when he was very young, the sensation was paired with a sense of something closing in on him like a lid on a box, that he was being trapped inside, now that he was older, just the sense of dread, with no discernible thought or memory associated with it.

What he didn't tell her, was the he knew it was likely a Post Traumatic Stress Disorder associated with childhood trauma he experienced at a pre-verbal age, a time when he could not yet consolidate procedural or episodic memories, times he only knew about because of stories he had been told, or the one photo that existed of him at that time, three years old and wrapped in a body cast. He had never told her any of those stories either. They would eventually come out, if she ever saw his body unclothed completely, but not yet.

The truth was that Chase lived in parallel worlds. The one he navigated when he was awake and the other, his dream world when he was asleep. A dystopian dreamscape of labyrinthian-like panoramas and rooms of complex intricacies, places he always navigated alone and almost always in a desperate and ongoing unsuccessful search for something he struggled to define.

She simply stated that she never had problems falling asleep and rarely if ever dreamed, though she did joke about snoring and farting in her sleep and asked if either would bother him when they lived together. She knew it made her seem cute, and the minor embarrassing disclosures would only endear herself more to him. While he thought he knew what she was doing, it still had the desired effect, in making him adore her more, and worry if her lack of dreaming was associated with her heavy nightly work-related drinking. He didn't probe and began to realize in hindsight that he shared much more about himself and his life than she did about herself or hers.

She never sent pictures with other men. Never once played that card. But she tested him in other ways. One night she mentioned being bar-fined by a British couple. "They brought me to their room to drink wine. Wanted me to watch while they had sex," she wrote. That was it. No elaboration. No context.

He stared at the message for a long time before responding: "I'm sure it was more than that."

She never confirmed. Never denied. Just replied: "Kha", which was her way of indicating that she wanted to change the subject.

He had learned that cue once after telling her a story about a fellow dancer who worked in her club who one night had sat on the couch next to him while she was onstage during one of her rotations and left an oily discharge on the seat when she stood to leave. One he was either too dumb or too curious about so he dipped his thumb in to smell to see what it was, thinking it might have been coconut oil, only to realize it was some vaginal discharge, likely from an infection. While she didn't come across as angry, her response made it clear the conversation was off limits. "Kha," was all she said.

Chase didn't know if it was avoidance or a warning, that some topics were off limits, or that he didn't have a right to discuss those realities of the world and profession she lived.

Meanwhile, Yuyi hovered like a memory in motion. Her scent, Chanel #5, still lingered on his shirts. Their time in Chengdu had been incandescent—meals at the rooftop cafe and elaborate breakfast buffet in his hotel, slow and quiet walks through the city at dusk, her body sliding beside his under the high thread-count sheets of their suite. The peaceful afternoons while he would play his electric guitar through the tiny practice amp he brought along on the trip, while she studied AI in online lessons on her phone. But it was her mind, her grace, her frightening ability to wield both seduction and softness that made him feel powerless in her presence. She was beautiful, of course. Devastatingly so. But she was more than that.

Yuyi was the full embodiment of feminine mastery. Every glance calculated. Every silence intentional. Every act of affection perfectly timed, and her sense of humor and ability to engage him in childish foolishness that had them both frequently laughing hysterically was magical. And it was how she never sought his validation, not like Yomiko or Julz, his women in LA, one insanely jealous, and both extremely needy and clingy.

One morning over breakfast, she looked at him through narrowed eyes, "You're different this time," she said softly, folding her napkin with precision. "Something is taking you away from me... little by little."

Chase put down his coffee. "Maybe I'm just getting old."

She smirked. "No, You're distracted. There's a shadow behind your eyes. You used to only look at me like I was your final answer. Now... it's like you're trying to solve for something else."

He reached for her hand. "You're still the most beautiful woman I've ever known."

Yuyi didn't pull away, but her eyes darkened with caution. "That's not an answer." His response was too good she thought, "Jealousy doesn't play well with you Darling, as we both know it's unattractive", said with a bit of a cocky smile, not quite a smirk. While she hated the response, she couldn't help but admire it, and in that moment, he was more attractive to her than he had ever been before. But she knew, he was slipping away from her, unless she did something to pull him more fully and completely back into her orbit. She had to think of the approach.

Back in Patong, Fern had begun noticing things too. One night, Fon came back to the room, tossed her bag on the bed, and without looking at her said, "He didn't come one night. Only night he's missed. And it just happened to be your night off."

Fern paused while applying makeup. "So, that was weeks ago, why do you still bring it up?"

Fon shrugged. "So, nothing. Just observing. He's not as dumb as most of them. Careful. Strategic. That's not good for you."

"What do you mean?" Fern asked.

"I mean," Fon said slowly, "you're already too close. You think you're the one with the plan. But you keep forgetting the rules change when you start to care."

Fon went on, "the look you have when you are texting and messaging back and forth with him is different than when you are doing it with the guys that are your actual sponsors." "You don't smile when doing it with them, but you do with him. You look goofy, like a school kid with a crush. Stupid".

Fern didn't reply, but inside her stomach tightened.

One night, after her shift, Chase's name lit up on her screen.

Chase wrote: "Can't sleep." "Me neither. Thinking of you," Fern replied. "You know what I miss?" he asked. "Tell me." She answered.

"Your thoughts and the way your mind works. The way you held me on the bike like we were already something."

She stared at the message for a long time. Then wrote: "We are something. Just not sure what yet."

She hesitated. Then deleted it. Typed again. "You are something to me, you are my everything, my beginning and my end." It was a canned line she had used before, taken from some movie or some AI generated line she had pulled and used in the past. It always had the desired effect, she knew it was exactly what they wanted to hear when they first expressed vulnerability in wanting her for more than her body, or a night, or a holiday girlfriend experience.

Fon, from the corner of the room, shifted in her bed. "You texting your American again?"

Fern didn't answer.

Fon turned her head, eyes sharp in the moonlight. "He's not going to save you. You know that, right?" "I don't need saving," Fern replied. Fon laughed bitterly. "That's the funniest lie we tell ourselves."

Neither spoke for a long time after that.

Fern scrolled up through her messages. Smiling. Hating herself for smiling. She still believed she was running the game. But she was no longer sure she was the only one holding the dice.

Chapter Nine

The Tension Beneath Still Waters

EVENINGS CAME EARLY IN Southern California. The coastal dusk had a calmness that belied the noise within Chase's mind. He would often walk the neighborhood streets after finishing the work in his practice, letting the ocean breeze cool the heat that Fern's latest message stirred in his chest. Most mornings now, she was the first thing he thought of. Most nights, the last. He knew it wasn't healthy. He knew he was losing the frame.

But he didn't care.

The truth was, he missed Thailand in ways he hadn't expected and hadn't in all of his previous trips. Not just the noise, the color, the heat—but the game. The constant low-level tension of decoding Fern's messages, trying to sense what was underneath. He missed the way she touched his arm just before getting off the bike. The childlike innocence her smile radiated in his direction when she thought no one was watching, when they would be out together, or the way he felt when she was in his arms in the club regardless of what was going on around them.

And he missed how her make-up would be on his towels after he washed his face, it having rubbed off on his skin while they made out together like stupid kids in the back of a car—small stains of intimacy, not what they really were, just a hustler's trail from the scene of a crime, like a blood trail a bank robber who got shot in the back while running way would leave. He'd look at them the next morning and feel something close to longing. Or maybe madness. He wasn't sure which. Stupidity for sure, that much he was aware of.

Yomiko was in one of her moods. She was always constantly fishing for clues he was fucking other women, and while she knew it, she didn't know for sure what he would get up to when he would suddenly disappear for weeks. Texting her from the plan as it took off, leaving her behind to wait for his return, seething, smoldering with anger and resentment.

It was the fact that he didn't seem to care if it pissed her off, that he didn't care if she walked, his nonchalance about their relationship, even after six years drove her crazy. She was obsessed with him, and for the life of her, couldn't muster the self-respect to leave him, to not just take what he gave her, no matter how much she pressured him, he wouldn't commit to her.

You fuck some slut in China, some Thai whore in Phuket she said one night, drying her hair after a shower at his place after they had just been together the way they always did when either one would go to the other's place on their once-a-week routine. She was picking the same fight she always tried to start, not being able to stand his ignoring her and his aloofness after they fucked, chasing conflict over indifference.

Chase didn't pretend not to hear, while he was busy working out some new riff from an old 80s Hair Metal song on his new Les Paul, he just responded in the same bemused, and over-the-top manner he knew in the ridiculousness of the response would defuse her anger and give her the drama and emotional charge she needed.

"Twenty cunts. I fucked twenty cunts that trip, 5 Chinese, 5 Thai, and 6 Koreans, those I flew in to bang three at a time. Ate their pussies, and fucked them, just like I do to you, you stupid Japanese slut, now shut up and either make me a sandwich or come over and suck my shriveled up little dick. If you're going to run that mouth of yours, at least put it to good use."

It didn't matter that the math didn't add up, the imagery, and the fact that he included Koreans in the mix gave her the charge she seemed to want. Sometimes he mixed up the Koreans with Filipinas knowing her complete racism and hatred of all other Asians besides Japanese would do the trick. It was a pattern that seemed to repeat between them regularly.

"Did you meet someone in Thailand?" she asked, trying to sound casual as if she had regained her composure. But it wasn't casual, it was desperation.

He hesitated. "Whatever" was his classic response, which she knew meant yes, but the conversation was over. After seven or eight years together, she knew he wasn't going to open up to her or become less detached.

But she pressed. "Was she a hooker?"

"All women are in one form or another" was his response.

Yomiko exhaled. "Why you fuck those trash bitches, Chase?"

"Because I like it dirty, cheap, and casual, and be glad I do, or you wouldn't be here. Now are we going to the movies or not?" And with that she seemed satisfied and responded with her classic "of course." And that was it, for now. He was hers for the night, and if that's all she could guarantee, it was enough. It had to be.

Fern's messages had changed. Longer. More frequent. Still seductive, but now lined with something rawer, needier. The night she told him she was going to Phi Phi Island for a week with a customer, she called it a "mission," and never alluded to if he was a long-term sponsor or some new guy she had just met in the club. The fact that they were going for a week suggested he was a sponsor, but Chase never pushed the issue or asked any questions knowing intuitively that probing came across as low-value, needy, anxious and insecure. He had also considered that in addition to her job at the club, she may also work for a service that hooked up guys with holiday girlfriends, it didn't really matter. In the end, it all turned his stomach and it hurt.

He wanted to not care, and wanted just as much to appear to her as if he didn't. He reflected, would he even be attracted to her if he met her working in the place, he took his laundry in Phuket once a week, and not in a Go-Go Bar? Her ass for sure would have caught his attention, but would he have been attracted to anything else? He didn't think so, and he made note of what that meant about him. He would need to process and integrate that further.

"He's married," she wrote. "Has kids. He's too clingy" but didn't expand on what that meant and Chase didn't respond or ask what she meant. He let her double and triple text. "I'll miss you so much. I'll think of you every day."

Chase's stomach twisted. He stared at the message before responding: "I understand. Be safe."

He lied. He only understood from a practical and matter-of-fact standpoint. The deeper truth was that while he didn't hate it, it caused him to struggle to hold on to the respect he wanted to have for her. It forced him to acknowledge that she was a whore, not some romantic figure overcoming an impoverished background, but a simple prostitute who chose the life to make as much money as possible, to exchange her dignity for fast cash and a party lifestyle. Or at least that is what he thought. The truth was he wasn't sure anything he knew about her background was actually true or not. He only knew what she told him and it was probably all bullshit.

When he thought about it carefully, what she told him didn't track. Why would a normal person with a Bachelor degree in Engineering and a normal 9-5 job working as a laboratory analyst quite to become a dancer and escort. The answer of more money didn't make sense. From his work years ago with street kids in Hollywood, those that engaged in survival sex, the term used by the kids who prostituted for a place to stay or for money to eat, or drugs, he knew the reasons were often much deeper, psychologically based in severe trauma. There had to be more to her history then she was telling him that she wanted him to know. What she was telling him had to be the version of her life she thought he could or would accept, but not the real truth.

It was the Puella Eterna in its embodiment and he knew it mirrored his own unwillingness to fully accept the lack of perceived freedom that comes with the responsibility of a truly integrated conventional adult life. He also knew if he lashed out, she'd win. So, he said the right thing. Cool. Detached. Controlled. She wasn't going to tell him what she didn't want him to know until she was ready, if ever, and pushing for details wasn't going to work with her.

She texted once or twice during that week. Discreetly. Short messages like: "Miss you Darling." "Wish I was with you," and the ridiculously absurd "mission almost complete, be home soon."

Like what she was doing was some sort of act of espionage, rather than being some married guy's whore for a week. He forced himself to accept that was her version of reality, not her euphemisms. He knew what working girls did with their customers. Essentially, anything they wanted, and usually what their wives or girlfriends back home wouldn't do. He shut it out and lied to himself that it didn't matter. He was diminishing himself to keep her in his life and he resented himself for it. It forced him to realize he was more fucked up than he had ever wanted to admit.

He didn't believe the words in the messages from her. He didn't re-read them, and he tried not to let them haunt him. He told himself that mastering jealousy was strength. That emotional discipline was masculinity. That true mastery came from being fully emotionally detached, that somehow, they could both compartmentalize what she was doing for a living, its effect on her psyche and soul, if she still had one, and somehow maintain a bubble world around themselves where none of it mattered. But he wasn't being honest with himself, because it did matter. It hurt, because he cared about her and wanted to see her as more than what she was showing him she really was.

He had learned to do that in the past, when he was the not-so-secret lover of a rich surgeon's wife for seven years. The woman lavished him with expensive gifts - a laptop computer, nice clothes, meals at high end restaurants, trips to Vegas, and both Del Mar and Santa Anita where she funded his gambling. Sure, they split the winnings when he won, but always ensuring there was plenty of cash and no cares if they didn't.

She even had the audacity to send her maid, her and her husband's maid, to his house to clean it every week, and shop to stock his refrigerator and wash his clothes - things he never even asked for - as long as he took her to bed and gave her the experience she wanted. She even paraded him in front of her girlfriends, showing him off to them, and lavishing affection on him in front of them. It taught him something about women, lessons he would never forget.

That went on for years, and he didn't mind, thought it was okay, rationalized it, even though he didn't need any of it. It was consistent with how he had been brought up and while he never mistook it for love, he allowed himself to justify it, until the day her husband confronted him in his office - a broken, shattered man, who for years had no idea his wife was fucking around on him with Chase, going behind him and their three kids backs for easy sex and companionship, all while he worked his ass off to provide her and their family the best possible lifestyle, and why?

All because early in their marriage she told Chase he had betrayed her for a short time with a scrub nurse from the hospital where he worked, and when the woman pressed him to leave her, he got stupid and didn't set clear limits, and when she showed up at their house and it got physical between her and his wife, and the police arrived and he didn't side fully with his wife. She was getting hers back and using Chase to do it, and he didn't care, it didn't matter to him, or so he told himself.

Was he a bad guy? No, Chase didn't think so, and in the hour, they had a conversation in his office when he showed up under the pretense of being a new client, Chase, realizing he hadn't come with a gun, quietly invited him to sit down and talk. Chase hadn't pulled any punches, or deny anything, in fact, he admitted everything and offered up that he didn't think he was the only one she was fucking, even offered to take a selfie with the guy, which he accepted, so he could show her that they had met in person and that her game was up.

Chase sent the poor bastard on his way, as if he had just made a new friend, convincing him that he was the least of his worries. Empathized with him, stating that while he understood it was "cheaper to keep her" then to divorce her, and helping him to see that he had much bigger problems with her than Chase was for him. The final blow was when he asked Chase what she told him about how she felt about him, and Chase answered honestly. "She tells me I am the love of her life." The look that came over his face in that moment was one of complete destruction. That was the truth about women, and Chase had learned it the easy way, but things in life are rarely easy and usually come back around on you, in one way or the other. He knew Karma was a bitch that would one day catch up to him and he wondered if Fern was going to represent things coming full circle somehow.

Did any of that help him rationalize what Fern was doing with her life and to make a living? Somehow allow him to relate to her on some level? He wasn't sure, but he saw the familiar similarities and it's what he found he told himself as the only way to keep from falling.

But there were cracks.

She returned from her trip and went silent for a day, then flooded him with messages. A full day of texting. She was on her two-day break and had been thinking about him non-stop, she said. She described wanting to be with him, wanting to leave the bar life, fantasizing about the life he described.

"I can be kitchen helper," she said. "I just want to be near you. Help you. Make you laugh. Make you happy. Take care of and protect you." "I will change for you, Kha."

Chase read it slowly, carefully. Then typed back, "I don't want you to change. The smart move is to keep dancing until I retire. We'll both be free then. I'll be making enough money by then that neither of us will ever have to worry."

He wasn't lying about that, with his pension and the passive income stream he was creating, he would likely die with a net worth of between $15 -18M. None of those specifics he shared with her, that would be telling her far too much as she already knew too much.

While he knew it wasn't the reply she wanted. He knew it was the truth. They needed time. He needed distance. Perspective. She didn't push back, but he could feel the shift.

Later that night, she wrote, "I've never had a sponsor. I never keep in contact. Too annoying. Too much work." He stared at it for a long time.

"Bullshit", he thought. She was too sharp. Too well-practiced. He knew a rehearsed line when he saw one. And it insulted him that she thought he might believe it. He didn't call her out, but he noted the weakness. The story she tried to sell, he wasn't wrong in giving her high intelligence the esteem it deserved, and since he knew he was right, he knew she would be, should be, had to be collecting as many sponsors as she could hope to manage. It was the only smart thing to do. And with understanding all of that and piecing together other details of her story, something in him hardened.

It was like the story she gave him to explain the scar from the C-section she had. She said she had served as a surrogate for a couple who could not conceive, and that while she had a child, its DNA was not hers. She expected him to believe that. If true, and it was doubtful, she truly had found a way to monetize her body as she claimed she was richly compensated for it. He played along, praising her for "giving the gift of life" and being " a source of light" for others, but inside he knew she was full of shit and most likely testing to see just how fabulous and incredulous a story he would believe. He understood that when telling lies, best to be audacious then conservative, and he realized she too knew that as well. She had admitted once, probably when her guard was down, that she was obsessed with money, and that was the truth.

The real truth had to be that she had a kid her parents were watching in Issan, that she was supporting through hooking and stripping, and she knew one those truths alone made her extremely damaged goods, and both made her completely undesirable by any guy who had his shit together. No Thai man would every want her if even one was true, but Farang were different these girls knew that, and perhaps she was hoping Chase was one of those who could accept one but not likely both. She couldn't lie about being a whore, that's how they met, but she probably calculated she could lie about having a child. She had no way of knowing if he would care or not and probably was just hedging that he would.

The next day, she sent photos from the Sea Scape House Cafe and Art Studio in Patong. One showed her holding a small canvas, smiling brightly. It was a painting—crude but recognizable. A depiction of their beach walk in Kamala from that first night.

She texted, "I painted us. Remember this night?"

He smiled, despite himself. He intuited the move, as probably an old hooker trick. A token of sentimentality to make the Farang feel chosen. Special.

It was effective. It worked. He didn't reply right away. He let it sit. Hours passed.

When he did, all he stated was, "I do remember. I remember everything."

She replied instantly, "That makes me happy. You make me happy."

Back in the room, Fon watched Fern from across the bed. "You sent him a picture of the painting?"

"Yes."

Fon shook her head. "You're in too deep." "Do you think it will matter to him, that the trick will work on him?" "You think he is that stupid? I don't think so."

Fern didn't respond. Just stared at her phone.

"He won't be your savior," Fon added. "He might not even come back."

Fern whispered, "I don't need him to save me." and silently, to herself she thought, "I just need him to want to." She rationalized to herself that she could either fleece him like all the others or just cut the cord and let him go if and when she chose.

Fon looked away. There was something ominous in her silence. Something dark and something calculating.

That night, Chase lay exhausted in his bed after a 16-hour work day, his phone beside him. No new messages. Just the photo of Fern holding the painting. Her smile too perfect. The brush strokes too simple. But the feeling it summoned was complicated.

He remembered how she held him on the back of the bike. How she smelled. How she fit against him. He remembered the makeup stains on the towels and how he would look at them the next morning after having held her in his arms the night before in the club all those evenings. He remembered everything.

And somewhere deep inside, he hated that he did.

Chapter Ten

A Smile Too Sharp

THE COUNTDOWN HAD BEGUN. Chase marked the date of departure on his office calendar, not in ink but in memory. He'd fly back in one month. And this time, he wouldn't be in and out. He'd be in Phuket for a full month—a regular gift he'd planned to give himself after another grueling half-year of dual work lives: by day, a civil servant coasting beneath bureaucratic radar; by night, operating a clinic to see patients in order to maximize the income he could invest.

His plan was simple: Rawai Beach. A small furnished apartment across the street from the ocean, he had found online, close to the quieter beaches, far from Bangla's neon claws. Fern would be on her two-week holiday from the club. They had talked about it vaguely, then more seriously, then almost like it was already real. The remainder of his stay, he planned to keep open-ended. His arrival would overlap both their birthdays—his at the end of April, hers in the middle of May. The hottest time to be in the Land of Smiles. Just fourteen days apart. Something about that had made her giddy, as though the universe had stamped them compatible in ink.

One morning, she sent a flurry of texts: You Tube videos of a Farang and his Thai wife on a hydroponic farm in Chiang Rai. Happy. Sunlit. Crops. Chickens. While she never explicitly said "We can do like this. I help you. I plant. I clean. I love." the future fake was implied. Chase had laughed, not at the idea, but at how perfectly she understood what he would want to believe—that simplicity and devotion could be real. He knew the move well, it was his go to play, and now it was being run on him.

But when he asked, "What's your actual plan for the future? What do you want to do when you stop dancing?" Letting her know that he had researched the shelf life of women that work as Go-Go dancers and learned that the average dancer retires from that line of the work at about the age of 35, no longer able to compete with the younger talent, something he said lined up with his own plan to retire as it gave both her and him exactly three years. She demurred. "Business maybe. I not sure yet. When I know more, I tell you."

He flagged it. Another *Puella Eterna* moment—forever young, forever floating, forever deferring responsibility for the future. Chase didn't push. He knew the signs. He had studied the behavior. But knowledge didn't grant immunity, and it also didn't mean she didn't have a plan, a woman as smart as her would, but that she didn't want him to know it was the most likely reality.

Then came the new drama.

"Last night police come," Fern texted. "Customer not pay drink bill. Big problem. Manager very angry."

Chase raised an eyebrow. "He ran a tab?"

"Yes. Big one. Over 6,000 baht. All girls drink. He refuse pay. Say we cheat. Police take him to jail. I have to talk to police, tell what happened, no problem for me but for the club."

He thought about it. At her club, they didn't let you run tabs. You paid as you ordered. Every drink. Every lady-drink. Always. That's how the racket worked. So, this story didn't track.

"The cops are going to kick his ass and he'll still have to pay," Chase replied. "Everyone knows the game. You argue, you lose. Always."

"Yes," Fern agreed. "But now manager watch me. Say I not sell enough drink this week." Chase couldn't remember if she started telling him about her nightly drink count or if he had started asking, once he knew that she had a quota to meet.

That was a new theme. They had started talking about her nightly drink counts. "Only six drink tonight, Kha," or "I not meet quota again. I worry they fire me."

He watched it unfold like a play. Not once did she ask for help. Not once did she ask for money. Instead, she leaned on the emotional pressure points. Fear. Stress. Insecurity. He admired the technique, but part of him wondered if she even knew she was doing it. It might have been reflex by now. He turned it into a way to show pride in her determination, and would tell her when she exceeded her count, that it was because she was the best, pushing the images of what he knew she had to do out of his mind, rubbing cock, lap dancing, more, to keep the customers engaged for extended periods, or would reassure her when she missed her mark by saying, something like "hang tough my intrepid little renegade" or more simply, "don't sweat it kid, you'll get them tomorrow night". Staying optimistic, reinforcing the inner strength and fortitude he respected about her. Her response was simple, "I'm determined". A refrain, he could only fathom the depths of what her "determination" would allow her to do, or what she was determined to get.

He had started referring to her with these nick names, referring to her as "Little Kid", "Tiny Dancer", "Intrepid Renegade" even once sending her a link to the song "Little Renegade" by Tuk Smith, but he wasn't sure if she liked them or not, she only once talked about his use of the word "kid" and sent him several pictures of her from childhood in her school uniform and standing with a group of friends. She knew she was adorable then, but demurred, saying her face was fat when he told her she was cute. He was seeing her for who she was underneath the façade, the inner traits that she possessed that were positive, it was validating for her, fueling her ego, but also touching something in her no customer had ever touched, and it drew her to him in ways she didn't want to accept.

Later that week, she texted from a pork BBQ stall after work. "I love pork BBQ. This is my favorite," she wrote, sending a blurry photo of skewers, red plastic stools, and Fon in the background. "I invite new girl from club tonight. She new here. Drink too much. I regret invite."

"Why regret?"

"She say too much. Loud. No control. This job not for weak heart."

Chase noted the coldness. The calculation. Fern saw people as tools. Or threats. Sometimes both. He wondered how she really saw him, and more specifically, if there was a duality to her view of him or, if more likely it was a one-sided hustler-mark assessment.

Meanwhile, in California, he kept up his routine with his Filipina Gik, Julz, a successful businesswoman who lived in a posh Townhouse in a nice neighborhood in Arcadia. They had fallen into a predictable pattern, as Chase needed an outlet every once in a while. Every couple of months, an evening together. Sex. A meal. Some rehashed conversation, her pressing him for commitment, asks about who else he was "dating", talk of their kids and plans to retire, how she was bitter towards her parents who only ever used her for money, and how no matter how much she sent or provided, it was never enough, always the same. Then he'd drop her off at her house and drive home, preferring to be alone, always refusing to stay the night. Julz usually pleading for him to come in and stay or have "one more go". "Why don't you ever stay over and spend the night? While she never stated that she felt he was just using her, the implications were there.

"Because I like my bed, Julz, And I don't like cuddling."

She pouted. "You like someone else now, huh? I feel it. I feel it in you."

He smiled. Said nothing. Later, she texted, the message coming in before he had even arrived back home: "I love you, even if you're cold. You always come back." He didn't reply.

At the same time, Fern texted: "What you doing?"

"Driving," Chase replied.

"Where?"

"I was seeing a Gik."

Silence. Then, "Drive safe, Kha."

It wasn't the first time she didn't ask a follow-up question. He could feel her withdrawing. Just a little.

A few days later came the veiled warning.

"You know, people watching on Bangla," Fern wrote one night. "Everything. They see who go where. Who talk to who."

"You mean the bar handlers? Or the other girls?"

"More. Eyes everywhere. I not let them hurt you."

That stopped him cold.

"Hurt me?"

"I not let them. I promise. I protect you."

"I can't fight what I can't see, Fern. If there are men behind you, I need to know that."

Her response was a delay. Then: "I never kill you."

He stared at the message. "What does that even mean?"

"Some Farang worry too much."

"I just don't want to get pushed off a balcony like in Pattaya" he stated warily.

"What mean pushed off?"

He didn't believe the confusion. It was too specific. Too staged. She changed the subject.

Two days later, he texted her, "I can't wait to be back. The moment I step off that plane will be the happiest of my year."

"I be there to meet you, Kha! I wait!" she replied, feigned childlike joy in her tone.

"Nope," he answered.

Several minutes passed. Then: "I have some business to take care of first."

"Ok, Kha."

She never pushed. Never crossed boundaries once he set them. That was what made her so dangerous. She respected his limits, but was always testing them, pressing gently around the edges, expert, far ahead of him at every turn.

It would often take him days to figure out her moves, which meant he was sure, that there were so many more she was making that he never saw, and couldn't know about. She, and this, he realized were on a whole other level, a league he had never played in, and one in which he was so clearly overmatched. He only had himself to blame at this point and he knew it.

And yet the game moved forward. One text at a time.

Each message a thread. A filament.

A web whose complexity he couldn't fathom, and one he wasn't sure he wanted to escape.

Chapter Eleven

Threshold

THE COUNTDOWN HAD BECOME a heartbeat. In the final days before his departure Chase's world narrowed to checklists, client wrap-ups, and meticulously folded clothes arranged in a suitcase he refused to overpack, despite knowing how quickly the unexpected could hijack control. Still, every move was deliberate. He wanted to arrive in Thailand not as a man escaping something—but as one prepared to face whatever waited.

Los Angeles felt drier than usual. Colder in ways that had nothing to do with the weather. He moved through his routines like a man in someone else's life, his hours spent counseling broken marriages and anxious professionals, while his nights were haunted by Fern's emojis and disjointed English texts that now felt more like signals than conversation. Most of his were weekends spent navigating the emotional minefield set out by Yomiko's insecurities. What could he say, he loved that Japanese MILF pussy, and had come to need it once a week or so.

On Thursday, Chase parked his car in a graffiti-scratched garage near Hill Street and walked into the downtown LA diamond district. The sales guy had slick hair, too much cologne, and eyes that understood desperation. Chase asked for nothing too flashy. Classic, clean, elegant. Something that said permanence without shouting ownership. He chose a 2.05 carat Ideal Cut, Color E, VVS clarity—an ice-clear promise.

"It'll appraise for nearly double," the salesman said as he sealed the velvet box.

Chase nodded. He did the math in his head. That was more than Fern made in a month, possibly two, depending on her quotas, bar fines, and tips. He tried not to think about that.

He didn't tell her about the necklace. Not yet. Timing was everything. A gift like this wasn't transactional, not for him. He didn't want to cheapen it by offering it too soon. It wasn't payment for companionship. It was a declaration—one he was terrified to make. But it would also be a way she could save face, providing a guy a holiday girlfriend experience in the eyes of her friends, without actually getting paid for it in cash. He didn't want her to walk away and feel cheated, he wanted her to know he cared about her and understood the difficult situation he was putting her in, and he rationalized that he wasn't really paying for her time in the classic sense, or so he deluded himself into thinking.

Text Threads & Subtext

Fern's messages came in like clockwork:

"I finish work, Kha.""Only sell 4 drink tonight.""Manager look angry."

He responded with encouragement. "Tough crowd tonight, huh?"

Sometimes she replied with memes. Sometimes with photos of pork BBQ from her favorite after-work street stall. "This make me happy. I eat with Fon."

Then came the edge.

"You exercise today?" he asked one morning.

"I dance 4 hour every night," she shot back. "You think that not count?"

She followed it up with a photo of her knees wrapped in tiger balm and towel compresses. "Need massage again. Too old already."

She was thirty-two. Not old by any traditional measure. But in her world, she was playing a younger woman's game. And she knew it.

One night she messaged, "I stay in room. Rest day. Watch movies." Then listed the titles—some Thai dramas, a few romantic comedies, a revenge thriller. It read like a mixtape of loneliness. He didn't comment on the theme. She didn't ask for his opinion.

Then another story.

"I go get dinner. Walk Bangla. Tourist throw fruit. Hit my face."

"What the hell? Are you hurt?"

"No bad. Just shock. I stay in room now."

He wanted to call. He wanted to hear her voice. But they had never spoken. Not once. A single accidental call weeks ago resulted in a fast message: "Roommate sleeping. No talk now."

Too convenient. But plausible. The way most lies were.

Drama & Power

A week before his flight, she told him about a fight between dancers after a post-shift pork BBQ dinner she had organized. "New girl drunk. Say bad thing. Another girl slap her face. Big drama."

"Who slapped who?" Chase asked, trying to decode her phrasing.

"Not me. I stop fight," she said.

He wasn't sure. The story shifted. He got the sense she was gauging his reaction—would he be protective? Would he see her as a victim? Or, worse, see her as someone capable of violence?

Then a few days later: "I must go early to club. Meeting."

Later, she told him the real purpose. "Manager say customer is for bar. Not girl. If customer buy drink, no fight. Just be happy."

A chill went through him. He pictured them lined up and lectured like soldiers. Reminded of their place. Of who controlled what.

"Must be hard," he texted.

She responded quickly. "Is job. I never have problem. Man want to buy me drink, next night, want to buy for other lady, I find different customer. No problem." She was making it clear that she didn't get emotionally invested in her work, that she saw everyone who came through the place as an object to fulfill a purpose, communicating that she was professional and detached. Was she trying to convince him, herself, or both, that none of it really mattered, that it was just a job like anything else people had to do to make a living. He didn't know if she was opening up, or what to make of it all. Would she fight for anything he wondered and remembered back to the incident where her roommate took her money and she didn't do anything about it. He was getting the sense that she avoided conflict at all cost, which tracked with her underlying personality of avoidance and detachment. The float above it all mentality that allowed her to stay in control and disconnected.

He also recalled how she had told him on at least two occasions that he could be honest with her, if he found someone better than her, she would understand, and just walk away, happy that he had found someone better than her, and that all he had to do was to tell her the truth. The significance of what she was saying hadn't really registered. He wasn't sure if she was showing a deep sense of insecurity and self-doubt, as that was not the façade she portrayed but perhaps it was real. It was possible that she never felt worthy of love or of his love, and he didn't appreciate then what those feelings could lead her to do to feel safe and to protect herself.

Packing & Pretense

Two nights before his flight, she messaged him that she was staying in that night to pack because she was so excited. "I pack now. Very big bag. Hope not problem."

"As long as it fits in the taxi," he replied.

She laughed. "I think you overpack."

Then, tentatively, he asked, "Have you ever stayed at that hotel before? With a customer?" He needed to know if the staff saw her as a working girl. He wasn't sure why it mattered. But it did.

"No," she replied. "Never stay there. Only you."

He didn't ask again. But he realized he was dancing around the edges of issues that were important and would potentially, eventually, need to be addressed and worked through and if they were going to have something together. What he didn't realize, but should have anticipated, would have anticipated, if he had not been walking into this with blinders on, was that the type of intimacy he was wanting from her may not have been something she was able to provide.

Fon's Intercept

Fon watched Fern pack from across the small room they shared. Her tone was quieter than usual. Calculated.

"You really go with him?" Fon asked.

Fern didn't look up. "Yes. Two weeks."

"No bar fine? No commission to club?"

"It's my holiday."

Fon folded her arms. "Club doesn't see it that way. If you're off books, they still track."

"I don't care."

"You should."

That night, Fon went to the manager. Quiet. Strategic. "She's going with the Farang. Not reporting. Not paying. Thought you should know." While Fon was employing her machinations, Fern reached out for wisdom, guidance, a counter-point to the toxicity she was surrounded in at work.

She took a walk and found herself sitting on the small red stool beside Pom's noodle cart again, her arms folded tightly over her chest. The heat rose off the asphalt in waves. She hadn't eaten a bite yet. The soup in front of her steamed gently while Pom, her hands moving with quiet expertise, ladled more broth into another bowl without asking if Fern wanted it.

"You've been quiet," Pom said, her voice low and even. "Usually means one of two things: trouble at the club, or trouble in the heart."

Fern didn't answer right away. Then she sighed, brushed a loose strand of hair behind her ear. "He asked me about my future. What I want to do in five years."

Pom raised an eyebrow. "And you told him?"

"I said... I live my life one quarter-mile at a time."

Pom stopped mid-stir. "Like in the car movie?"

Fern nodded, wincing. "He laughed. Said I was too smart to live my life based on lines from cheesy American films."

Pom chuckled, but there was sadness in it. "He's not wrong. That kind of line—it works in bars. But with a man like him, if you give a shallow answer he won't think less of you, but you might start thinking less of yourself."

Fern swallowed. "He makes me see myself different. Better. I think that's part of the problem."

Pom nodded slowly. "That's because he doesn't want to change you. He wants to see you become what you already could be. That kind of man's rare, Fern.'

She knew what the old lady was saying was true, and it added to her fear and self-doubt.

She knew he was wrestling with trying to find a way to fit into her life and a way for her to fit into his, but for as much as he thought he knew, he didn't really understand how things worked for women like her. She had tried to help him see, but feared she would come across as only wanting him for his money, and while that may have been true at the beginning, she had slowly wanted so much more.

He couldn't understand that for her to go with him, and not come back with compensation was putting her in an almost impossible position, and even if she paid her own bar-fine, the vulnerability emotionally it created for her was almost as intense, because it would mean that she was fully trusting that he was being honest and sincere with truly wanting her for something real and not just a holiday girlfriend experience. He was asking her to shift between her professional and personal personas, something she swore she would never do. An idea that had always terrified her.

Her professional persona was her ultimate defense, a mask and roll she had built over years of cultivated effort to create an impenetrable boundary between the dangers of relationships with anyone in the real world, and her heart. She could never trust anyone in the past to protect it, so now why did she think he would. The world of illusion she lived in, was the only place she ever felt safe. The thought of it was overwhelming her.

Departure

In the lounge at LAX, Chase sat with a drink in hand, the velvet box tucked deep in his carry-on. Fern had been texting non-stop.

"I so excited. Never meet my boyfriend at airport before. Like YouTube video. Like love story."

He hesitated. Then wrote: "We're going to have a great time together!" The reference to him as her boyfriend stood out, but he didn't bite, but wondered.

Pause.

"I hope you have safe flight, not problem. I want make coffee for you every day, you hold me at night when we sleep. Travel with you. Just you."

He reread her words a dozen times. Wanting to believe them. Needing to.

The boarding of his flight was announced and the gate number lit up on the screen. He finished his drink and headed towards the lounge exit. He tucked the phone into his pocket and walked towards his gate. Toward her.

Toward the part of the story where everything would either unravel—or become undeniable.

Act Three

Chapter Twelve

The Garden Exit

Phuket International Airport – 11:37 AM

CHASE WAS GRATEFUL THAT his connecting flight from Hong Kong to Phuket had him sitting in the first row of seats, as it meant he could be the first-off the plane and the first from the flight through Customs. He was eager to resume where they had left off, excited to see her, knowing that she was going to be there to meet him pleased him even though he knew it was an easy way for her to build credibility. It nevertheless added to the girlfriend experience he had wanted to have and even more wanted to believe could be real.

The hum of the escalator beneath Chase's shoes was drowned out by the thrum in his chest. Even now, with the worst behind him—passport checked, bags scanned, customs cleared—his breath ran tight, clenched beneath the anticipation. He had imagined this moment more times than he could count: Fern waiting with eyes that searched for only him, rushing into his arms, the kind of cinematic reunion he had no business hoping for. But wanted anyway, for as much as he didn't want to admit, it was emotional moments like this, the buildup and release of tension, the mystery and intrigue of a romance, even if contrived that drained the boredom, the mundane from life that most people just accepted, but which he, even pushing fifty-three, refused to accept. If it meant this, at least for now, then so be it, anything was better than the grind of staring at his computer monitor, or having to play the office politics at work. He refused to allow his life to only be about that, and for better or worse, he was about to continue an adventure he had started six months ago.

His phone buzzed. "I'm here." Followed by a photo of the Amazon Coffee kiosk just past baggage claim. The message had been waiting for him when his phone picked up reception as the plan descended into the Phuket airport and taxied towards the terminal. Yet, when he looked up as he rounded the exit from baggage claim and walked towards the coffee café, she said she was waiting at. Nothing, and as he stood there for a moment, he wondered where she could be.

He lingered at the doors, the swell of the crowd shifting around him, a steady stream of tourists moving by him and out into the balmy Thailand heat, all starting adventures of their own. But no Fern. "I don't see you," he texted back, making note of his frustration, and the irritation that comes from having been in transit for the last 20 hours, and for having to wait for someone, even if it was her, the minute he landed in what for him had become what Disney Land, Knotts Berry, and Six Flags all rolled up in one were to a 10 year old boy about to start his summer vacation.

A pause.

And then—she emerged. From outside, not from inside the café' like he expected, but from the bright light of the world just outside the terminal's entrance. She moved in a slow semicircle, not a straight approach, a kind of sidelong arc that felt more instinctive than spontaneous. She was smiling, eyes bright, and in her hands a bouquet of white wildflowers—simple, but sweet. He had wanted to see her initial reaction when she first saw him, evaluate it, he had learned to pay attention to that initial reaction, that first image when the person you were either meeting or waiting to see had when they saw you, as it could tell you so much, and what he observed was telling.

She approached like someone who was excited but cautious, hesitancy overridden by interest. Not running, not rushing. But careful. Like she was gauging his emotional altitude to see if she was safe. That curve in her walk—he'd seen it before. Not in a woman, but in a dog. His daughter's rescue mutt, when she was still terrified of men, circling slow before trusting the space. The memory hit him harder than he liked. Sure, she walked with a quick excitement and a smile like she was elated to see him, but the way she was looking sideways and walked in the arch, not straight and directly too him said something, and it wasn't the innocent, and unadulterated excitement someone had for another they had longed to see. It was something else, he was sure of that. The smile was real, but beneath it, there was fear or caution or a gauging of him like he was doing to her.

He stayed where he was. Didn't reach. Didn't smile. Let her come to him. His eyes well hidden behind Rey-Ban Wayfarers. He wanted to maintain control and the edge of her approaching him rather than he rushing to her, validating her, after all, it was he who had flown thousands of miles to get there, not her.

Fern thought instantly, that he looked... colder. Still. Not angry, not excited. Just... watching. The way a man watches a card dealer before deciding if the game is rigged. She hated that look. Made her feel less in control, like she was going to have to work harder than she had planned or wanted to, and at the same time was robbing her of the fantasy that he was swept away by her, that maybe he hadn't yet fully decided if he *wanted* her. This wasn't the scene she has watched played out on the YouTube videos of lovers being reunited, this was calculated, and it resonated.

She softened her face, kissed him—brief, tender, but without pressure—and pressed the flowers into his hands like a peace offering. No bag. No overnight clothes.

"Where's your stuff?" he asked. "I not stay yet. My holiday start in two day. I check in with you first, okay?"

Changed already. The plan. The tone. The choreography. Still smiling. Still pretty. Still in control. He gestured toward the taxi stand. Didn't argue or press the issue. But he didn't like the feeling it instilled, the uncertainty about what it meant, the confusion it created.

She had gone outside to avoid the air conditioning, she told him and showed him where she had been sitting and staring, waiting for him just outside the glass as they moved out of the exit and towards that taxi stand. Showing him the condensation on the inside of the glass she had repeatedly cleared so she could have a better view from the outside in, smiling as if she thought her discomfort with the airconditioned interior meant something endearing.

She suggested that they get a Grab taxi, commenting that the cab stand would charge him at least 200 Baht more than the App would charge but quickly deferring to him when he indicated he didn't care to pull up the service on his phone as he peeled off the 700 Baht the taxi stand driver requested, from a stack of what looked like around 10,000 baht already in his pocket.

Cab Ride – 12:05 PM

The cab smelled like stale cologne and old plastic. They sat close, not touching, her smiling up at him and him looking at her, unreadable through his dark glasses. She leaned in close, resting her head on his shoulder and acting surprised when she asked "music" hearing the sounds from emanating from arm of his sunglasses. *Starry Eyes* by Motley Crue was playing as he pulled the glasses off to show her that they not only played music but also had the ability to shoot still photos and videos from small lenses located on the front of the frames. "Oh, how much they cost?" she asked. "Don't know, they were a gift" he replied matter-of-fact, without elaborating that they were from Yomiko, and she didn't press for who had bought them, instead opting to tell that him that the management of the club had discussed their emergence on the scene and how to handle the situation if customers starting showing up wearing them. There was a strict "no filming" rule in all the clubs and non-compliance with those rules was strictly not tolerated. He smiled and said, "Yes, I won't be wearing them when I come to visit you at the club."

As they approached Patong, Fern let out a low-pitched "Uh oh" when the driver swerved to avoid a scooter. It was the voice of a child trying to make a moment cute. "Uh oh," Chase echoed, but there was no warmth in it, more a dry recognition that she was in character, and despite how adorable she was in the role, he was surprised at how disarming it was, and how easy it was for him to let down his guard. He realized two weeks alone together, day and night, was not going to be easy psychologically, because he knew he couldn't ever let himself be unguarded.

She texted quickly in Thai. Two out, one in. Fast fingers. Fast thoughts. She had been told to let Fon know when he had arrived and they on their way back to Patong, knowing why they were concerned, and still figuring out in her mind how she was going to navigate the mine field that lay ahead of her if she was to actually spend two weeks alone with Chase as anywhere in Patong was wrought with danger of watching, observing, and reporting eyes.

It would have been so much easier if he had just agreed to meet in Bangkok, where the two of them could have blended naturally and unnoticed into the bustling crowds of that great city. But he hadn't wanted to, and when he had pressed the issue, her culture and instincts were to defer to the man and not argue or become demanding or insistent. She sensed his concerns, the unreadable angles, and that combined with what she was coming to understand about his natural wariness, made her question why she was even moving this forward with him at all as she continually told herself she was putting in too much work, and beyond expecting, was *hoping* for far too much.

He wasn't looking at her. Not really. Not the way he did last time. Back then, he watched her like he was learning about her. Now, he watched like he was confirming suspicions. He had seemingly lost the boyish innocence she found so simultaneously disarming and appealing, yes romantic even. How could it have been replaced within the last six months with this coolness, and did it mean she had overplayed her hand, given away too much, or even worse, been misreading him all along, or was he simply trying extra hard to appear as if he was in control. She convinced herself it was the latter and allowed herself, for the last remaining moments of the car ride to be at ease, the plan that would follow from the time they got to the hotel had been laid out in advance. Worked out and dictated to her by Fon and the manager, and perhaps even a few higher in the syndicate than themselves, even she couldn't know that level of detail for sure though she had her suspicions.

She was in character. Already. That sweet tone, that baby-doll trill—it wasn't the Fern he wanted, it was the Fern that was. It was the "whatever the situation calls for", the professional. The one that made drunk men believe in things they should've outgrown. He hated how much it still worked on him, and how easily he found himself with his guard down despite his best efforts to stay focused. She was simply that good, or her ways fit to closely with his wants and needs, he wasn't sure, but he knew, like a wrestler realizing that they were beaten before the final third tap of the referee's hand on the mat, he sensed he was in for more than he could possibly bargain for.

Hotel Check-In — 12:30 PM

The concierge's practiced smile didn't waver, but the moment hung. Fern dug through her small wallet fishing for something she already knew wasn't there, going through the motions, working the charade. "I forgot ID... Only have photo on phone. I go get it, okay? Just ten-minute. I be right back"

He nodded, calm. Too calm. His surprise, annoyance, and irritation well hidden behind the façade of coolness he had worked to cultivate since before even getting on the plane. While he had gotten much better at mastering his response to these types of unpleasant emotions, it was all the more difficult when he actually cared, and in this case he obviously did, still he stayed composed, responded with "no problem" as he sat back in the chair and feigned disinterest and nonchalance as the hotel staff bowed and stepped away, likely having seen similar routines like this playout regularly. The disappointment had started, as he had wanted them to check in together, like a real couple on vacation, not what it really was, a working girl and a customer. Even if he hadn't paid for anything from her, it was how it was perceived, and it mattered to him because it stripped away the illusion he had built in his mind, and that disappointment hurt.

CHASE

She didn't forget. No one in her world forgets that presenting an ID is required. It's mandatory. This was a move. A retreat. A test. A power play. He wasn't sure which. But he knew for sure, that she was aware of the need to present her ID when checking into resorts like this even if she is not the guest paying for the stay. That it is a mandatory requirement of the hotel in order to protect the paying guest from any unscrupulous working girl who may otherwise rob their customer while on their premises. When she showed up with him with no luggage and him clearly there for a long stay, she had to have known they would know she was just a short-time "guest" of his and would demand she provide proof of identification at check in.

He watched her leave, didn't tap his foot, didn't look at the time. He let the performance run. While she was gone, he sat back and waited and tried to determine the real reason she was making this move. Did she want to communicate clearly and unequivocally to the hotel staff that she wasn't "staying with him", that they "weren't together" and that she was nothing more than a casual friend or short-time girl?

Then why hurry back to her room to retrieve and then present the ID, he couldn't figure it out, but no way it was an oversight on her part, no way in Hell. Perhaps it was her way of telling him that she didn't want to follow the plan they had talked through without simply coming out and saying it directly. It didn't matter. The message was clear. *We aren't really together.*

She returned nine minutes later, as promised. Not flushed, not breathless, but smiling like nothing was wrong. Typical Thai style.

They checked in, and were escorted to the room, but the fact that she didn't bring anything she would leave in the room, should have told him all he needed to know, namely that she never planned to stay with him, but he was either too tired from the flight, or just to slow to pick up on it at the time.

Flashback – Two Weeks Ago, Bar Manager's Office

"She going off books?" the manager asked when Fon had approached her again with her concerns about Fern. While the manager considered why Fon was in front of her again with this. She didn't really care, as she had learned to stay as much above the daily drama that unfolded between the girls as possible as long as it wasn't threatening to impact their work. She knew all too well that with these girls, drama was as regular a part of their daily lives as shitting was to everyone else, and who had time to be concerned about when everyone in their orbit took a shit?

Fon didn't flinch. "Says it's her holiday and nobody cares what she does when she is on her own time. But she met him six months ago in the club, and now he's back." She went on to seal the deal by stating, "she and him talk twice a day, but he not her sponsor, and they have been planning this the whole time."

The manager leaned back, exhaled a stream of smoke. "Then she better come back with something for the club, cover her bar-fine for the two weeks. Or she doesn't come back at all." She let Fon know that her and Fern were to report to her office on the night the Farang returns if he does end up coming back, and she tasked Fon with keeping her eye on things and letting her know, or it would be on her as well. Fon nodded quickly and smiled inside to herself as she backed out of the office and went back to their room upstairs. She had been in the game the longest and had played it at the highest levels, and there was no way she was going to be the one left with nothing. No way at all.

Hotel Room — 1:00 PM

The cold towels were folded like origami on a tray. She peeled one open and, sitting beside him on the small sofa as the staff moved his bags in and explained the amenities and the swimming pool rules, and when the breakfast buffet opened, she began wiping each of his fingers like it was a sacred ritual. Not rushed. Reverent. She even dropped to one knee in front of him and helped him slip off his shoes, hands soft but firm.

It was too ceremonial to be casual. He couldn't tell if it was cultural, emotional—or psychological warfare dressed in caretaking. While he knew instinctively to allow her to assume the feminine role, he couldn't help but sense that it was overdone and a bit too theatrical even for SEA standards. He was used to the woman here, dotting on "their man" manicuring them while sitting at a table having beers, massaging their neck and shoulders while lounging by the pool, or whatever, but this seemed above and beyond.

As he quickly unpacked, he handed her a few gifts: in rapid waves—carefully selected: a cropped, pink I LA tee shirt, the same style worn by the protagonist in Revenge, her favorite movie; a Sick Bitch brand tee, hat, and coffee mug. Trinkets with an edge, a persona in cotton and ceramic. Tools, maybe, for play-acting domesticity.

She lit up with childlike delight, especially at the Sick Bitch set. She put the tee shirt and hat on immediately, striking poses on the edge of the bed, holding her phone up for selfies, smiling with the innocence of a schoolgirl. The same smile as those old photos she had sent months ago—legs tucked beneath her, hand to cheek, eyes tilted up as if caught in wonder. But Chase noticed now: the angle, the lighting, the expressions. The same. Practiced. Echoes, not spontaneity.

He remembered. She saw it in his eyes—that flicker of recognition. He was too sharp to miss the mimicry, but he said nothing. Still, she felt the shift, and found herself feeling momentarily off guard. The spell not broken, but thinning. She pressed harder, smiled wider. Staged another playful kiss in front of the mirror. *Keep it light. Keep it sweet.*

He reached into his bag again and pulled out a boxed chess set. She tilted her head, puzzled. He handed her his phone, the screen glowing with a quote:

> *"Chess contains the concentrated essence of life: First, because to win you have to be supremely patient and farseeing: and second, because the game is built on patterns... In chess as in life, when people cannot figure out what you are doing, they are kept in a state of terror—waiting, uncertain, confused."*

—Robert Greene, The 48 Laws of Power

She murmured thanks, low and soft, then sat cross-legged on the hotel's tiny couch, fingers delicately moving the wooden pieces around in their velvet lined place holders underneath the board. She traced the knight's curve with her thumb. Studied the queen. Her smile had dimmed, the edges of her lips tightened. He noticed that she was deep in thought.

So, this was what he thought of her. A strategist. A player in the game. Not a lover. Not a muse. A calculation. A pawn that might act like a queen when needed.

She didn't hate it. Not entirely. There was a strange power in being seen so clearly and still having the upper hand. But it stung, too. Because he hadn't kissed her. Hadn't claimed her. Not once. And yet he expected her to open up like a flower in daylight.

She looked up once, caught his gaze. Held it longer than she intended and thought to herself:

You want to play games, Chase? I've lived them. You read about patterns—I breathe them. I've had to. That's what no one like you ever understands.

But she smiled. Just a small one, and caught herself saying in her manufactured elevated tone "thank you" as the words were only partly out of her mouth, her routine was too predictable, he had spotted and identified her plays, she would have to change strategies, perhaps *reinvent herself,* and fast if she was to retain tactical advantage. She wasn't aware of the sadness in her eyes in that moment, and he didn't understand it either.

He had envisioned teaching her the game and them spending hours together over the upcoming weeks playing together, something unique that they could share, but the intent behind the gift had clearly been missed and he could tell she wasn't interested in the game. She misread his gesture and it would have to go unspoken, hanging in the space between them like a contaminant in the air.

As he finished semi-unpacking, she noticed as he lined up four sets of new sneakers, all similar but all distinctly different enough to complement different looks and different attire, along one wall in the room in a meticulous almost obsessive manner. He changed his clothes quickly, brushed his teeth, rinsed his mouth, and announced that he was starving and they had to get something to eat, not because he was going to kiss her passionately and ravage her on the bed like she had expected, almost hoped, but because he wanted to leave, as if being in the room finally alone together was anxiety provoking for him. She was disappointed and turned off, and found herself wanting to put space and distance between them.

No, it was definitely time to change tactics, he was not letting her sexuality control him, he was not giving himself the chance, or her the chance to make him weak by succumbing to his desire for her, he wasn't willing to give up that power and control to her yet, and it made her question again if he actually *wanted* her. But there was a deeper truth behind his lack of sexual aggressiveness with her.

He was intimidated by her work, the sheer number of men she went to bed with on a regular basis. He wasn't afraid of measuring up as much as he was concerned that the act, at this point couldn't possibly mean anything to her, and he didn't want to experience the realization the first time he thought he was making love to her, that she was dissociated, detached, not really present but just going through the motions, and he hadn't figured out in his mind yet how he was going to navigate those waters if he found himself in them. He thought, that over the upcoming two weeks, their togetherness would spur on a more natural exchange, and that consistent time together would better help ensure a warm and organic experience, that she could be real if given time to feel truly comfortable. He had no way of knowing what she thought about it deep in her heart, and that was unsettling to him, and it represented just another confound that existed in their situation that went undiscussed and unresolved in his mind.

At the restaurant, after they had decided what to order, she teased him by saying "Pineapple fried rice not real Thai food Kha."

They laughed. A moment. But only that, and while she made sure to share her entre with him, after he had spooned a healthy portion of the fried rice and chicken and red curry on her plate that he had ordered, they didn't talk about much, both seemingly lost in their own thoughts.

At the bar they went to after lunch, the same one they had their second date at and one Chase was clearly familiar with and comfortable in, they played Connect Four. She beat him cleanly and quickly the first two rounds. Lost the third by just enough to be obvious, making one of two things clear to Chase, that she either already knew how to play well before the six months ago when he thought he had showed her the game at that bar in Kamala Beach, which was more likely, or she had learned the pattern she had spoken about back then that she intuited was the secret to easy victory every time, or that someone taught her, or maybe she studied it and had an experienced bar girl show her how to win. He wasn't sure if it bothered or flattered him if she had actually taken the time to get good at a game that was not a part of her work life, knowing how much he liked it.

He noticed. She could tell. He was always clocking her. Never resting. Even when he smiled, she could tell that he was thinking, processing, analyzing, strategizing. She was both flattered and threatened. With every other guy she delt with her entire life, what they wanted was simple, singular and obvious. They wanted to possess her body, the first ones back when she was still a an actual child, wanted to take her true innocence, then later and most recently the ones that came and went, who wanted to experience the feigned innocence she had mastered the ability to depict, mostly for a few fleeting moments, hours, perhaps a week or so at a time, but few if any, and certainly not on the level Chase appeared to want, to possess her mind, to understand it, to get inside it, appreciate it. Control it?

She glanced at her phone. Another message. She didn't reply. Then a phone call she took and spoke briefly to the caller, her mother, she offered when she saw him glance casually at her between shots on the pool table. Then it came time for her to head back to her room to get ready for work as she only had about an hour and a half before her shift was to start.

As they walked back along beach road, they stopped briefly to watch a beach volleyball match underway on Patong Beach. Fern commenting to Chase about how funny ladyboys can talk, following a quick conversation she had with one who was playing in the game they had stopped to see. Then, as they continued to head back in the direction of Bagla Road, after having crossed beach road to the other side of the street, she stopped abruptly, asked a food vendor something in Thai. Then turned to him, eyes unreadable. "You go back to your room now, okay?"

He blinked. Nodded. "Okay." It wasn't an invitation. It was a command. It was a dismissal.

And just like that, she turned and walked away, not ahead of him in the same direction, but in the opposite direction from her room and where he thought she needed to go. He didn't stop her, question her, or follow her, but did stare and watch as she walked away and out of sight before turning back towards his room, clearly confused and uncertain as to what she was up to or where she might be going. Thoughts raced through his mind that she had possibly set up a short-time customer, a quick blow job and/or screw to make some fast and easy money before work or just as likely, that it was simply a disorientation tactic to jerk with his emotions.

If it was the former, he knew he had no right to ask how she spent her time, and if it was the later, it left him unsettled that they had to keep playing these games. He reminded himself to man-up, not care, stop acting like an emotional wreck and get and keep his head in the game, though it was a game he was quickly wishing he could take a time-out from, and all this and he had only been in town for a few hours.

It also reminded him, that he really wasn't okay with how she earned a living, no matter how much he tried to convince them both that he was. Truthfully, since he had met her and they had gotten involved with one another personally, he was walking through a gauntlet of almost daily assaults on his feelings, leaving him hurt, confused, and disoriented. Some the result of tests, others based on the simple reality of things, all combined with a lack of clarity on how any of it would or could change if they were to actually decide to build something real together.

Back in the room he undressed slowly, mind spinning. Was she punishing him? Testing him? Or going to meet someone else?

Sleep found him late. Uneasy. Shallow and restless. He woke frequently and quickly went back to sleep despite being wracked with unpleasant and disorienting dreams. When he finally awoke, somewhat refreshed he showered and reminded himself that he was back in Fantasy Land and should get busy enjoying himself regardless of what did or did not shake out with Fern.

It was close to midnight when Chase finally found himself standing at the Currency Exchange at the Beach Road entrance to the Walking Street on Bangla Road. After exchanging three hundred US to Thai Baht, he smiled to himself as he started his slow stroll up the street, his senses immediately flooded with stimulation, sights, sounds, and the smells he had all come to associate with this place, a place he always longed to return to. He found himself fighting that same familiar pull to go straight to her club, and he hoped, to her waiting arms.

He realized that strange paradox of their developing relationship, and while the last six months of regular text communication and brought them closer together emotionally, at least in his mind, it dawned on him that he only felt comfortable with close physical connection in the confines of the club, a fact he hoped he would have the opportunity to sort out in the upcoming weeks together.

But rather than going straight there, he made his obligatory stops in several of the other Go-Go bars along the strip, having a few drinks and noticing at one place in particular, the line-up of girls appeared to have completely changed from six months prior when he would go in before ending his night at Fern's club. He noted, the turn over and wondered if Fern's claims and concerns about the lack of stability in her job may be real, or if it simply reflected the naturally high turnover rate at these clubs in general and wondered what it may mean for her stability in the profession or at least at her current establishment.

At last, he couldn't resist any longer and he made his way through the velvet curtain at her club, three hawkers and door men fighting to open the door and usher him in as usual. When he stepped inside, he saw her immediately to his right, almost on top of him as he entered, he looked out, trying to appear to scan the room as he waited momentarily to see what she would do. She wasn't dancing. She was waiting. Watching the door, or so it seemed and she immediately approached him, with a warm hug and greeting. To which he responded with the canned line he had rehearsed in his mind over the last six months of waiting for this moment. "Hey kid, want a drink?" or something similarly pathetic now in hindsight.

They went straight to their usual spot on the couch in the center of the room and picked up where they had left off six months earlier, she kissed him like the past five hours didn't exist, he noticing her breath did not smell like mouthwash, the tell-tale sign she had already been with a customer. He bought them drinks between her sets and they made out like before, slow, deliberate, sensual. She moved on him. Slow. Skilled. He noticed that she kept her eyes open sometimes when the kissed deeply and at other times she would have them closed. When both of their eyes were opened, they would stare into each other's, and he wondered what she was really thinking, as he would slowly caress her neck, back and legs with slow deliberate motions. He wondered if she liked it or if she thought it felt creepy, like the hands of a decrepit old man, like the guy sitting him next to them on the couch rubbing a twenty-year old's clit through her bikini while another, slightly older girl rubbed his cock through his shorts.

Chase reminded himself that Fern did that every night of the week, and that what she was doing with him in that moment tonight was nothing new to her, and that even if it mattered to him, it couldn't possibly, not a chance in Hell, mean anything different to her than it did any other of those hundreds of other nights when it was other guys in his place. The fact that it felt like it did to him was evidence of two things and two things only, she was that good, and he was easily susceptible to the right set of charms, and while it didn't really matter in the end why she possessed the ones she did, when compared to the countless other girls who had no effect on him, she did and he had to accept that and not go weak.

But he had gone weak, and the six months of regular texts, and seemingly loving communications between them couldn't and shouldn't mean anything other than an experienced operator had found a suitable mark, and this time, he was not that operator and she was not that mark, she was that operator, and he was that mark. Period.

"I want to see your face," she whispered as she straddled his lap, cupped his face in her hands and bent in to kiss him deeply, smile beaming, while pushing her crotch into his and pumping her hips rhythmically.

This wasn't a performance. This was something older. More dangerous. The kind of moment that made men forget logic and give up entire lives. Because it was performance, and because it had a firmer, longer foundation, only meant she was much more in control and he in a much more of a vulnerable position than he would have ever wanted to let himself otherwise fall into. The simple and plain truth was that he was never in control, not even a little, and he knew it. That's why what happened next was predictable, textbook even, and something he should have saw coming from a mile away and yet it blindsided him like sucker punch thrown in the dark.

He let her know he was leaving about an hour before her club closed, not wanting the end of her shift, his presence and them being seen leaving together without him bar-fining her make things awkward or risky for her. They agreed to meet up and grab dinner. So, an hour later when he messaged her that he was hungry and that she should 'hurry up", he wasn't surprised to get her typical after work text message.

3:30 AM – Birthday Text

"Happy Birthday to the Prince Charming of my life. Today, I'd like you to know that you are the most special person in my life and will always be so. May you be blessed with infinite love and happiness."

It was too polished. Too flowery. Grammar perfect. Voice unfamiliar. AI, probably. Didn't matter, he was half drunk and did not have his head in the game at that point in the night. He was used to these sorts of admissions of love on her part even if they were not typically so grammatically correct. Besides, it was what he wanted to hear, which made it so much easier to absorb.

He replied anyway. Asked if she wanted food.

"With my roommate. She wait me." Was her response. They met a few minutes later and the three of them jumped into a Tuk Tuk, that hustled them up to some late-night spot that served Thai food off of the third road.

When they got seated, Chase picked up on the change in mood and tone that had characterized the earlier part of the evening when they were in the club and it was all love and affection. Now, it was qualitatively different.

Fern sat on Fon's side of the table, not next to Chase, he sat alone across from them. After ordering their food and Chase saying how it was nice to meet Fon and her nodding and exchanging the pleasantry, nobody really spoke, and Chase, sensing something was awry, but not knowing what, remained silent, watching as Fern, normally voracious, picked at her food, and chewed and swallowed slowly, almost with a morose melancholic manner to her eating. Fon never said another word to Chase and only sporadically spoke with Fern and always in Thai. The silence was no longer shared—it was weaponized.

They were performing now. But not for him. For each other. This was a ritual sacrifice. Something had already been decided. But Chase hadn't pieced it together yet. When they left and jumped into a Grab taxi Fon had apparently ordered, Fern sat in the back next to Chase but did not lean against him and hardly spoke, if at all, and when he leaned his arm against her twice, he felt her noticeable and inexplicable withdrawal immediately. Something had shifted. They were both up to something, because, even if Fern had decided something, Fon should have been more talkative, even if only with Fern, the fact that nobody said anything meant they were both in on it. Like in the mob movies when everyone knows one amongst them is going to get whacked, except the guy about to get popped behind the ear.

As they pulled up to the entrance to Bangla Road Fern turned to Chase and said, "I see you tomorrow at 2:00 pm, taxi take you to your hotel." "Ok" was all he remembered uttering, as she climbed out without so much as a kiss on the cheek.

He didn't really remember getting back to his room or thinking much at all, confusion, alcohol, and exhaustion from almost 30 hours of travel and emotional intrigue had him spent, so he had to have been asleep when the next series of texts came into his phone.

The first one immediately deleted at 6:09 am. Then the second and last of that night, at 7:18 am, another polished, obviously AI-generated message that read *"Tomorrow I have something I want to talk to you about, and I'd like to bring my roommate, Fon, with me. Will that be convenient for you at 1:00 pm?"*

What had transpired in the 15 minutes between her first flowery loving message where she professed her undying love, and the time they met, where the tone had clearly changed, was a mystery that Chase knew he would never really understand.

Chapter Thirteen

Into the Forge

May 1st – The Garden, Patong – 2:00 PM

THE MIDDAY HEAT PRESSED down on the island like judgment. There was a kind of stillness that seemed to have settled over Phuket and a silence that to Chase felt less like peace and more like a verdict.

Chase walked slowly, deliberately, and stepped into the garden not knowing what he was walking into but sensing something waiting for him that had been orchestrated in advance to keep him off balance and to catch him with his guard down. After the invitation to meet that morning had come, he thought they were going to ask him for money, a loan of some sort, help them fund some type of business, a restaurant or bar maybe, and he had thought through his response. He wasn't ready for what they actually had planned however, and though it should have been as obvious as the day was hot, he didn't see it coming.

"Hey," Chase said, as casually as he could.

Fern nodded. Her eyes didn't sparkle today. No schoolgirl poses. No smile tucked behind a coy glance. Just a tired kind of sadness, and something else. She looked frail, tired, broken, her hands in her lap and shoulders slouched forward. Resignation.

"I need to talk," she said quietly, but not looking him directly in the eye, yet.

He sat, struggling with the strength to pull the chair out from the table to sit. It was wooden and heavy, and felt like it was actually made of iron, and it scraped faintly against the patio tile as he pulled it out, the sound grating on his nerves. "What's on your mind, Kid?" as he nodded acknowledgment in Fon's direction. She nodding back quickly but not making eye contact, furtively retreating her attention back to her phone scroll.

Fern's lips trembled, then steadied. "I want to end our relationship, Chase."

Chase didn't believe it. Not entirely. Fon's presence was more than emotional support. It was surveillance. A handler. An anchor. But it didn't matter in this moment. Now he needed to know why. Her statement had caught him off guard and his hurt and confusion gushed out-"Why, what's changed?"

"I'm worried, after last night, can't focus on my work and you. Too hard." was her explanation. "So, you are worried, that means you are afraid, is that right? he asked in response. "Yes, I scared too." "You would rather throw something good away rather than live with the worry that you could lose it?" He asked. She simply repeated "I need to focus on my work for now," tears running down her face, lips quivering and shoulders hunching even more, starting to turn her body unconsciously in Fon's direction for emotional support or anchoring.

Chase remained calm, didn't get emotional, angry, tearful, simply stated in a matter-of-fact way as he removed his Ray Bans so she could see the tiredness, disappointment, and hurt in his eyes. "My assumption is that you have thought this through, and it's what you want, that you've decided, and that's it." It was a response he had prepared in hindsight and had waiting in his toolkit for any type of power play like this should he need it, though never suspecting that it would be drawn upon today, with her, now.

She nodded, tears flowing off her face, turning reflectively towards Fon who appeared as disinterested as ever, scrolling on her phone but clearly taking the whole thing in. He fumbled his words trying to tell her that regret was a worse feeling to live with than was failure, implying that to give up without trying was the bigger mistake, but he saw her tuning him out and turning her gaze to Fon. He stopped trying to convince her, stopped trying to talk her into something good for her and away from a life-changing mistake. It wasn't the time and she was not a receptive audience. He was only diminishing himself with every word he spoke. And he didn't think she was actually listening or even hearing what he was saying. She was checked out and he could tell, emotionally drained.

The whole interaction lasted just a few brief moments. Six months of connection undone in a few brief moments and a few direct comments. To her credit, she was clear, unambiguous and concise. She didn't waffle, wasn't vague and didn't leave things ambiguous or open ended. It was over, and it was what she wanted, even though she appeared in agony and completely distraught. Not at all like someone who was about to get something the really wanted. But Chase knew accepting was the only thing he could do that would not diminish himself and his worth.

He paused briefly, letting the moment hang, then with resignation, stood and said before turning to walk away "Up to You, as the saying goes." and he walked to his room, not looking back, but the image of her, sobbing, lipstick to heavily applied and cracked in strange lines, and body seeming frail and tiny in the large chair. Fon seemed inflated, full, and victorious. The drama was well done on both of their parts, like two veteran actresses who had just pulled off the main scene in a movie they had both been cast perfectly to perform in.

Later, he would replay the moment—the tension in Fern's jaw, the flick of Fon's eyes whenever Fern hesitated. The flowery AI-sounding birthday message from just twelve hours earlier now stank of strategic placement. A decoy. A sugar-coated distraction dropped in before the blade, or a heartfelt goodbye. He couldn't tell which.

And what had changed? On the surface, none of it made sense, but the game wasn't being played on the surface level, as Chase was used to, as he had been playing it. The game she was playing, was deeply layered, complex, and sophisticated. She had always been several moves ahead, and he playing catch up, his moves not ever really mattering to the direction things were moving in, or the current, or ultimate final score.

It was also possible that for Fern, *Love* was both as beautiful as it was terrifying. Perhaps a withdrawal was a survival tactic, necessary to return to a place of emotional equilibrium and safety. That made sense too. Her need to feel in control and not emotionally vulnerable could lead her to sabotage their opportunity to have something deeper than a superficial relationship, and that was something she was not emotionally ready to navigate. He guessed that he would never know. It was however consistent with her psychology, the *Puella Eterna* complex, longing for a romantic and idealized love, but unable or unwilling to allow herself to be vulnerable enough to sit with the fear of being hurt and losing it that could only be possible if she gave up her sense of control and need for safety. Avoidance was her defense, and when cloaked in an illusion she could control, it had become central to her persona.

Was she wrestling with the pull between her need to hold onto a staunchly independent identity at the cost of having something deeper, real love, or had she lost attraction to Chase, and simply decided to cut things off out of disinterest. While it didn't seem likely, he had to acknowledge he hadn't played this right from the start, letting his desire for her cloud his judgment. Now he would never know and he had to live with the uncertainty of wondering if she ever felt anything for him at all. He also had to wrestle with the inevitable self-doubt that crept in around the edges while also taking responsibility for the situation he had allowed himself to embroil himself in.

The other possibility, the one most likely after all, was that she simply was not willing to exchange her currency for romance or a shot at love. That she may have either had a better offer for her time, one that actually paid, or that she wouldn't or couldn't allow herself to be with any man who was not a real customer. If the relationship was like a poker game, every time she checked her hand to him, he checked back, never committing any chips to the center of the table, never giving her anything she really valued to win, and at some point, when she realized he was playing with "scared money" she stood up from the game to find a table with players who were willing to bet big.

Fern thought to herself: "I couldn't do it. I wanted to. But then I showed her the message."

It had started just after her shift ended. She'd gone back to the room, showered quickly. Still dizzy from the emotion of the club and the alcohol, from what she let herself feel—too much. She sat on the edge of the bed, staring at her phone, then typed the birthday message. The original was shorter. Simpler. But Fon saw it.

"He waited six months," Fon said. "You need to make it count."

Fon had suggested edits. Then handed her another phone. Better grammar. Softer tone. More beautiful.

Fern had copied it. Sent it. And it felt good. Like telling the truth without using her own voice. She deleted her original.

But when she saw Chase at the restaurant that night and sat across from him—silent, guarded—she hated herself. She felt false. All of it felt false, and while she knew she was being strategic, doing the logical, smart thing, she questioned if she couldn't just be real, trust that his interest in her was genuine, that what they had, what they had talked about having, what they could build, could be real too. But that wasn't the way these things worked in Thailand, that wasn't how it was played, that wasn't what happened in the end to girls like her. The retreat to a detached state of control and distance felt safe, even if like surrender, and that safety was alluring. It also squared her with Fon and the managers. That pressure would be relieved and those problems solved.

Others were now calling the plays, and the game had gotten more complex because her feelings had gotten involved, and out of line, and now both were being pulled back in line regardless of what she may have truly hoped for or wanted. It was a consequence of being controlled, owned, a part of something bigger than just herself. Because when parasites rely on you, what you decide or think you can decide impacts them. She needed them, but they needed her too, the complexity of the dynamic demanded that she consider the larger system she was a part of, and she knew that was something he didn't fully appreciate, even if he had a rudimentary comprehension of it, because in his world, which was not as interdependent as hers, he couldn't truly grasp it yet.

Fon had seen it before. Too many times. Girls who got too close. Too hopeful. It always ended the same: broke and broken. If the girl didn't fleece the man, the man invariably broke the girl. Cinderella stories really only ever played out in the movies. The manager had already spoken to her twice. If Fern didn't deliver—if she didn't get a payment or at least a promise—she'd lose her place. Her shift. Her security. The interdependent nature of the business, didn't afford Fern the right to see him as hers. He, was the club's customer and if they were going to spend two weeks alone together in Rawai as they had planned, that simply meant he wouldn't be in the club spending money, and that simply was not how it worked here. If they wanted to do that, he had to pay her bar-fine for the two weeks, and then no problem. Didn't matter that she had two weeks leave on her books, it wasn't about her, and she wasn't going back to the village to see her family, she was spending time with their customer. She couldn't bring herself to pay her own bar fine, so that was that.

Fern

But what if he wasn't like the others? What if he was serious?

Still, the cab ride was agony. Chase was silent. His arm brushed hers once, twice. She pulled away each time without knowing why.

Because closeness meant risk. And risk meant loss. Creating an emotional distance manifested through physically withdrawing was instinctive.

She hadn't decided to end it until late that night. Not entirely. But by morning, the decision had calcified. Fon had helped script the message. Suggested the time. "Be soft. Say you scared. They always understand scared."

She typed the message. Read it aloud. Fon nodded.

CHASE (internal)

He heard it in her voice the moment she spoke. The performance wasn't bad. But it wasn't her. Not the her he remembered. Not even the one he knew might be a construct.

"I can't do this," she said. "You're distraction. I must focus. I think too much."

It wasn't just a breakup. It was a cutting loose. A severance, clean and cold.

He tried to negotiate, gently. Tried to bring her back to the texture of what they'd built—texts, shared feelings, the future plans they had talked about. He only realized later that creating a vision of a future together only reinforced a fear response, it didn't increase a sense of safety in her. In fact, it created the opposite effect, because it not only created a conflict with the Puella Eterna complex she had constructed her life around, but it drew them closer in ways that felt confining, increasing a sense of vulnerability that she didn't have the emotional skills to manage. It was possible that the only way she could let a man near her was if there was a financial transaction element to the relationship. He knew he would never know, and realized he never really knew her at all.

But she kept glancing at Fon. And every time she did, a little more of Chase slipped from her orbit.

He asked her one last time, "Is this what you want?"

She nodded, eyes full of tears but voice flat. "Yes."

He stood. Uttered something trite. Walked away.

May 2nd – Patong Hotel, Noon

He hadn't slept. Not really. Slept in patches. Dreams disturbed and more chaotic than normal. The room felt too big now. His unpacked clothing seemed ridiculous. His lined-up shoes. His cologne. The books he brought, that he planned to finish reading on the mornings he sat in bed while she slept next to him or during their afternoons after watching movies while she prepared herself for their evenings out.

He poured himself coffee into the Sick Bitch mug. Sat on the edge of the bed. And stared at his phone. No messages. No unread voice notes. Emptiness. Until they stopped so abruptly, he hadn't fully appreciated how much the regular and consistent text messages from Fern had meant to him. While he had always looked forward to them, craved them even, he didn't know then how much he would actually feel the impact of their absence when they stopped coming. He had become attached to her in ways he was only now starting to realize.

Chase thought ironically as if he felt sorry for himself. *The player got played*.

He should've known better. Should've seen it coming. And he had—but part of him wanted to lose. Wanted her to win. Maybe because somewhere in the seduction was the only place he ever truly felt vulnerable. Alive. A part of the reason he had started this whole thing with her was to make himself feel more truly alive, and he accepted that heartache was a consequence and he embraced it, almost needed it, like a cutter needs the pain to feel something, anything real. And yet the finality of it, the emptiness, it touched him deeply.

She wasn't evil. She was adaptive. A creature sculpted by trauma and necessity.

Still, he had questions. Why Fon at dinner and in the garden the next day? Why the AI generated message? Why the tears if the decision was already made and she was getting what she really wanted?

And beneath it all—why did it still feel like something had been left unsaid?

He would spend the next few days wandering. Drinking Thai whiskey in beer bars. Watching the tide come in and out. Reflecting. Not just on Fern, but on himself.

Fern visited Pom again, finding that after the unfolding events from the previous day, she needed insight, clarity, and reassurance that she was being smart. Over the past months she had grown increasingly reliant on the talks she had with Pom and now was a time when she felt she needed her more than ever.

Pom had seen the change in her young friend over the past six months. She had a brightness in her eyes and her smile was easier to come by or so it had seemed, but now, both had been replaced with an uncertainty, a sullen sadness that was noticeable. She opened: "You different lately Fern, what's changed?" Her response was short and had a despondency Pom had never seen in her before. "He's gone, I threw him away, and he isn't fighting for me like I thought he would, not like in the movies."

Pom replied, "Most men try to possess what they're afraid to lose. But a strong man—he lets go. He sees love as a choice, not ownership."

Fern looked down. "We talked once, about trust. If it's even possible for people like us. I told him something you once said. 'Distance proves a horse, time proves a man.' I told him it was Thai wisdom."

Pom smiled at that. "It is. And now you're living the test."

"He told me he doesn't have friends. Says he's alone most of the time. But... he's a good father. Paid for his daughter's college already. Never broke a promise to me. Not one."

Pom grew still. Then looked Fern in the eye.

"A man who can be alone with his thoughts is strong. He doesn't need noise to drown his doubts. You know that a man who is at peace when alone with just himself is confident—in the best way. Because he isn't trying to fill a hole. He's full already, and he doesn't need to prop himself up with someone else. He's secure, and when he chooses you, it's because he wants you, not because he needs you."

Fern was silent, her hands tightening around her chopsticks.

Pom said quietly. "You miss the way he made you see yourself. And now that he's gone, you can't unsee it. That's the wound."

Fern's voice cracked. "He hasn't messaged since I left him in the garden. Not once. He hasn't reached out asking for a chance, or for any kind of clarification. No one has ever disappeared like he has."

Pom nodded. "Because he respects your words. Most men would beg. He let you go, not because he didn't care, but because he did. Love like that doesn't chase—it waits. And it watches. And it remembers."

Pom leaned in. "Tell me something, Fern. What kind of man is he? Really. When no one's watching?"

Fern thought for a moment. "He... notices everything. Reads people. Watches. But he never uses it to hurt. He never made me feel small. Not once." She went on, "He was always trying to build me up, encourage me. He was supportive, understanding, and he didn't judge me. He knows what I do, and he picked me anyway."

Pom smiled. "Then you already know what you have to do."

Fern looked confused. "What's that?"

"Ask yourself if the person you are when you're with him... is the person you want to be. If the answer's yes, you better fight to keep that version of you alive—whether he comes back or not."

Pom went back to stirring the soup. Fern picked up her spoon, but her appetite hadn't returned.

"Sometimes" Pom murmured without looking up, "you must let go of people who aren't ready to let you love them, even if it hurts.' But if you're the one who wasn't ready, Fern... then maybe it's time to change that." Fern didn't speak. But her heart was loud in her chest. The few moments of relief she had initially felt when she cut him loose was now being replaced with a sinking, hollow, empty feeling of doubt and self-recrimination.

He'd come for the story. Got the ending. But maybe now—now came the rewrite.

He was being thrown into the forge. To be broken. To be burned. To become something else. Okay, fine, but something still didn't add up, somethings still didn't make sense, something was still off.

Chapter Fourteen

Rawai Alone

May 3rd – Rawai Apartment

THE TAXI RIDE DOWN to Rawai should have felt like a transition. A change of setting, a clean slate. But for Chase, it felt like exile. The taxi drifted through the southern curve of Phuket and he in it like a man carrying invisible weights. Music from her playlist melancholic in his ears, Camila's Consequences; now taking on a prophetic irony he had anticipated months ago when he had found the song after she had sent him a different song of Camila's, Never Be the Same, one day while they were texting when he told her that he thought he was addicted to her.

Prior to the trip, listening to those two songs had become a regular routine of his to break up the monotony of a day of working from home, and while they were small ties that created an illusion of closeness with her then, they were now just poignant reminders of what he should have avoided all together, had he possessed a less self-destructive nature.

The tropical breeze offered no relief. Everything was a blur—green jungle, tattered shop signs, the neon smile of tourist bars opening too early. None of it penetrated. Not really. Normally, on a ride like this, he would be clocking the girls sitting out in front of the beer bars as he passed, making mental notes of the ones he would plan to circle back to in the upcoming evenings ahead, like a hunter out spotting at night for deer, but on this day, on this ride, he wasn't spotting for his next conquest, he was contemplative. He had broken every rule in every book, and now, as predictable as the sun's rise and setting, he was being justly punished, and he let himself feel the weight of the self-inflicted wound, the self-inflicted lesson.

There had been no word from Fern. Not a text, not an emoji. Just absence. And that absence screamed louder than any confrontation ever could. He didn't expect her to reach out, definitely not this soon after having made her last move; no, she was waiting, the ball was his to play, of that much he was certain of. But all he could do was anticipate what she might think he would do, and then make damn sure that wasn't what he did.

The obvious play was simple, do nothing, just mirror her behavior and rather than chase, appear desperate, needy, or devastated, stay clear, give space, let the impact of her decision and the void it created in her life be felt. If anything was true of what she had said about how much he mattered to her, about how much their daily communications meant to her, then she should be experiencing a self-inflicted wound of her own making and the best thing he could do was let her have what she said she wanted. Him, no longer in her life distracting her, making her "worry", making her afraid.

Let her wonder if she had made the wrong move, let her contemplate if all her efforts over the last six months were going to amount to nothing, no emotional connection, no chance at a stable and respectable future, or in her world what was far more important, a quick financial windfall. If she really didn't want his love, or his presence in her life, he wasn't going to debase himself by trying to convince her to see things the other way.

In the Rawai apartment, he dumped his bag, opened the blinds, and stood staring out at the palms swaying above the pool. He was supposed to be here with her. Supposed to wake to the sound of her brushing her teeth, pulling her hair into a ponytail, asking if he wanted eggs. He poured himself a coffee she had promised to make for him every morning, and sat in silence.

CHASE (internal)

I was the mark. Or maybe just the experiment.

Still, it didn't make sense.

Why walk away now? After six months of carefully building the illusion, of deepening intimacy, of playing the long con with subtlety and precision—why sever the thread when the payoff was finally at hand?

He had arrived ready. More than ready. He had the diamond. He had the words. He had the willingness to believe. And she threw it away.

Unless...

Unless she didn't. Had he overplayed his hand, letting her know he was on a three-year plan to retire. The long con was just that, a long, drawn-out ordeal, that from what he knew about the way it was often played here in Thailand encompassed years, and layers of complexity and deceit and duplicity that most Westerners couldn't fathom.

In America, it would be unheard of, almost incomprehensible, for a man to let his wife sleep with other men for money, let alone go with them for years, get pregnant with their babies, ceremonially, if not legally, marry them, live together as man and wife for years, all while both living and siphoning off money to send to him and their kids, and set themselves up to eventually take everything. Hell, Chase had even heard of stories where the duped Ferang lets the Thai husband or boyfriend move in, having been convinced he is her beloved's brother.

They convince him to buy land and build a house, all in her name, only to come home one day to find her Thai husband there, and he gets run off with the threat of violence and a lack of any legal protection against the scam. It happened all time here, that and worse. Sometimes, it ended in a faked suicide, a man "jumps" off his hotel balcony with no apparent reason to take his own life, and security footage either "unavailable" or inconclusive. No, the long con here was just that.

In more benign situations, if you can call them that, a Westerner meets a "nice" Thai lady, develops a romance, they move into an apartment together, that he of course, completely furnishes with high-end appliances and furniture, only to come home one day and find that she has cleaned him out and disappeared back to her village with no real trace of how to contact her and a local police force disinterested in even trying.

Fern (internal, May 3rd)

Fon was watching everything. Her phone. Her messages. Even her silences. The fallout from the breakup was supposed to feel clean. Efficient. Tactical.

But it didn't.

She lay in her room, eyes fixed on the ceiling fan, phone pressed to her chest like it might hear her heart breaking. She wanted to text him. "Where are you? Did you sleep okay? Did you eat?" But she didn't. Couldn't.

Fon had reminded her that the window was closed. She had to move on. He hadn't paid. There was nothing to report. And chasing him now made her look weak. She chided her, rubbing salt into the wound, "he didn't even protest, didn't drag you by your hair to his room and take you...just let you go so easily." "Must not have really cared after all, *Teerac*," her last word said dripping with sarcasm and bitterness.

Weakness wasn't allowed, and was duly punished in their world. It needed to sink in, they are customers, and no matter how much you try to get them to believe otherwise, you had better never think it's anything more than that.

FERN (internal)

He should have fought harder. That's the truth. He should have said no. Pulled me aside. Taken me anyway. Not accepted what I said at face value. Doesn't he understand how this place works?

But then the other voice came in. The colder one. The survivalist, and Pom's words echoed.

You're projecting. He respected your words. That's what good men do. And good men get left behind or plead not to be. But strong men, men who know their value, their worth don't beg. You caught him off guard, and he displayed dignity, high value, self-respect. He didn't crack, crumble, fall apart, he left with his esteem intact. He made you an offer, and you rejected it, told him you didn't want what he was giving.

Still, she felt haunted by the way he walked away. By the weight in his eyes. Not anger. Not even betrayal. Just... hurt. Disappointment.

May 5th – Rawai Beach, Sunset

Chase sat on the seawall, nursing a Chang and watching the fishing boats drag themselves in on tired waves. He hadn't spoken to anyone in days. Not in any real way. The solitude had weight. It gnawed at him. But he welcomed the gnawing. Let it carve something new. Embraced the time and the isolation to learn more about himself, get stronger, both physically and mentally. Take ownership of the place he had gotten himself into and the work he would need to do to move forward.

He had come here chasing a feeling. Not Fern, exactly, but the feeling around her. The idea of her. The electricity of being close to danger wrapped in softness. Love as roulette. The high-stakes romanticism that made him feel alive. Initially he had wanted the challenge of seeing if he could break through her professional persona. See if he had enough game to crack her frame and pull her into his. Get her to really care about him. He never considered that he would get caught in his own web. He began to appreciate that passion tied to danger, intrigue, and chaos may be exciting, but it wasn't love.

And yet it happened. He missed her, and was hurt by her dismissal. By the callous way she had discarded him, and he felt both guilty and like it was a well-deserved lesson. He smiled sardonically at himself and muttered, What Goes Around Comes Around, seeing the karmic irony in what he had done to so many others over the years, finally getting done to him. The fact that he brought it on himself made it all the more poignant.

And now? Now he sat with the burn marks. Trying not to scratch. Trying to learn something from the itch as the burn started to scab over.

There were plenty of things in hindsight, he would have done differently. For one, he shouldn't have shown up at the club that first night, should have gone off and got drunk somewhere else, let her wonder where he was why he hadn't shown up, worry and go looking for him. Hell, he should have fucked her roughly as soon as they got to the room, and instead of going out for lunch and beer, ordered room service then made love to her for the hours before she had to leave for her shift, then not showed up at her club later that night and gone drinking by himself. But he knew that would just be a repeat of the same old patterns he was used to. While it may leave him in control, it would never lead to true intimacy. And he should have known to have not sought true intimacy with a working girl. Potential isn't a promise and shouldn't cloud one's judgment unless disappointment is an acceptable outcome.

Hindsight is a bitch sometimes, he thought to himself. All lessons learned, never be the nice guy, and perhaps that was his greatest take away, he was too much that nice guy with her and of course, predicably, she read it instinctively as weakness and now he was paying for it.

He told himself that she was probably sitting somewhere with Fon relieved and chuckling over having gotten rid of the old fucker, disappointed perhaps that she didn't make a score, but grateful that she wasn't going to have to try and navigate two weeks with his moldy old ass. Relieved to be done with him.

But the truth was, as much as he vacillated between self-doubt, over analysis, and recrimination, he really didn't know what had happened. It was the uncertainty that was as destabilizing emotionally as the abandonment he felt.

FERN (internal, May 5th)

She hadn't slept well since the day in the garden. Fon was pulling away, too—cooler, more distant. Her status at the club was tenuous. The manager had made it clear she was now under a kind of probation. She'd cost them. The story was she got too close to the customer and let him go without extracting what they were due, and those who had been watching had thought she had gone soft and let any easy mark get over on her, both to her and their detriment.

She wasn't sure if it was true. But it felt true.

She reread their texts from two months earlier. The ones where he told her about his past, his fears, his family. And the ones where she wrote things that weren't just part of the game. Weren't entirely lies.

The worst part? She missed him. She wasn't supposed to miss anyone. But the truth was, she had come to rely on their daily messages, and his supportive, encouraging, validating words, they built her up, strengthened her, made her feel good about herself, despite what she was doing to make a living, the degrading things were lessened by his acceptance and approval of who he saw her as underneath it all, and she hadn't anticipated what not having that presence in her life would feel like.

It had become like a drug, not one that numbed or depleted her like the large amounts of alcohol she consumed nightly, but like an Upper, that elevated both her mood and her spirit, at least what was left of it. She was beginning to realize that she was missing who she was in his eyes, the way she felt in the world that their communication had created, and she had not anticipated missing that, in fact, had not really noticed that it existed at all, until it was gone.

But she felt something else as well - shame, humiliation that she walked away with nothing. Not even an armful of shopping bags from a trip to the Central Festival, a new handbag, a bobble, hell, even a pair of fucking jeans. Nothing, and if he was gone for real, like she feared, the loss of face was inconceivable, she struggled to push the conflicting feelings out of her mind. She had repeatedly told him that she didn't want his money, and now, ironically, that was exactly what she wasn't going to get, not a single Baht of it. Six months wasted, with nothing to show but heartache. It wasn't supposed to have ended this way, and if she had anything to do with it, it wouldn't. She was after all, *determined.*

CHASE (internal)

Why did she need Fon at dinner? Why did the birthday text sound like it was written by someone else? Why end something that was about to pay off? None of it added up.

Unless she wasn't playing a game the way he thought. Or unless she wasn't calling the shots anymore. He couldn't stop the questions. And the questions were as bad as the loss.

He opened his notebook. Wrote down three words:

"The game changed."

Maybe she was in too deep. Maybe she had to choose them over him. Perhaps, she was being truthful, and was choosing control over closeness, safety over love. Or, perhaps after seeing him in person after six months, she just wasn't attracted to him and didn't want to waste any more of her time.

Or maybe, just maybe, she was waiting to see what he would do next.

Chapter Fifteen

The Crucible

May 6th – Rawai, Morning Routines

EACH DAY BEGAN WITH movement. A 10,000-step walk along the waterline, where the early morning tide exposed rocks like bones in the surf. Chase kept his earbuds in, but no music played, letting the noise canceling feature drown out the rest of the world. He liked the silence—it amplified the sound of breath, the pull of muscle, the rhythm of feet on sand. The body in motion dulled the chaos taking place in the mind, and the burning he felt in his chest.

By noon, he was in the gym. Slow reps. Deliberate form. The kind of lifting that built not just strength, but discipline. He didn't train for aesthetics. He trained for sharpness. For clarity. For the quiet pride of doing something hard while no one watched. The months behind his, desk and late-night work with his clients had pulled him into a sedentariness that had softened him, not just mentally but physically as well, and he used these vacations not just as a chance to recharge his mind and spirit, but to pull himself back into physical shape.

Then came the massage.

She was short and slim. Late thirties. Strong. Her hands moved through him like a surgeon—thumbs into calves, knuckles down the spine. Each stroke was brutal. She'd pause, to wipe sweat from her brow, and shake her head in disbelief.

"You no feel pain?" she asked, watching for the flinch.

He didn't move.

She tried harder. Knees, elbows, her full weight behind her hands. He stayed still, even when she put the full weight of her body on her elbow pushing as hard as she could, and holding it, then gyrating slowly into his shoulder blades, a technique most could not tolerate, but he never budged, never let out the slightest of grunts, groans or sound of any kind. He stayed motionless, and though she could only see his face in periphery, he never flinched, blinked hard or even closed his eyes. His stare, distant, his mind, his heart, were somewhere other than on the massage mat beneath him.

He only moved when changing songs on his phone, sad American songs, most she never heard before, but could understand enough of the words to know what they meant, and that they were touching something in him she couldn't reach with her hands, knuckles or elbows, no matter how much pressure she exerted.

She sighed under her breath. "You man with broken heart. I see some like you. You feel something else, not this."

He responded quietly as if from a thousand miles away: "This kind of pain doesn't hurt."

She thought more, "He's handsome and has money. Tall. Polite. Smells clean, like soap and man. But empty eyes, sad, still. He holds it in like secret. Like man in war. I see this before. Thai girl breaks his heart", and with that she smiled to herself, knowing he would be back again for what she could provide, what he needed, something physical to distract from the hurt that was crushing him on the inside and the war being waged in his mind.

She softened her strokes toward the end. Let the touch become something else. Less punishment. More healing, and she offered herself to him, she wanted see what he would go for and to see what he would be like.

She wasn't surprised when he responded physically to her touch and caress below, but at the gentle firmness with which he took her, holding her in his arms as he entered her, caressing the small of her back, thighs and breasts as he kissed her neck and ears, keeping his eyes closed as he made love, not fucked her. She knew it wasn't her he was responding too, but the her in his mind, the one behind the source of his hurt. Years in this business, she had seen it all, but this was somehow different, and for the first time in as long as she could remember, she didn't have to just tolerate what was happening and wish it would hurry and be over. Not that she let herself enjoy the interaction, that wasn't really possible, but it wasn't ugly, either.

May 9th – Rawai, Evening

There was another girl. One he met in a bar off the main strip. Young, soft-voiced. Bright eyes that hadn't gone dark yet. He took her home once—not for sex, but for something stranger: intimacy.

They sat on the couch watching a romantic American movie about a rich businessman with a bondage fetish and a romantic flare. He told her it was one of Fern's favorites. She didn't ask who Fern was. She just smiled and leaned her head on his shoulder, surprised when he later, during the movie, when the sex scenes started, laid his head in her lap and taking her hand, used in to caress his face while his thumb alternated between pressing her wrist gently (feeling her pulse quicken though she didn't know that was what he was doing), and caressing it and her palm, kissing both gently from time to time. She expected him to try and fuck her when the scenes in the movie got hot and heavy, but he never made his move, and when the movie was over, he said he was going to bed, returned from his room with a blanket, one of his tee shirts, and an extra pillow and said" you can stay here if you like and we can get breakfast in the morning or I can call you a Grab, up to you". She stayed. And the next day, when he dropped her off back at her bar after breakfast, she never asked him for money.

Now she messaged him daily. "You come see me?"

He rarely replied.

She sat in her room dreaming. Told her friends at the bar the next day, when they asked her conspiratorially about the hot American who had bar-fined her earlier the previous evening, that he was different. That he made her feel safe. That she thought he might come again. She waited.

But Chase was elsewhere.

He rode his scooter aimlessly. Up the hills behind Nai Harn. Down into Kata. He found cliff overlooks where the air thinned, and sat reading Jung, Greene, and dog-eared novels with broken spines.

Back in the apartment, he was in bed reading most nights by 10, asleep by midnight. Women from his life back home and elsewhere—California, Arizona, China, even one from the Philippines—messaged him. Some old sparks testing the flame, others less frequent visits in his rotation. He didn't chase. Half he didn't even answer.

He wasn't desperate for affection, and no longer seemed to care about keeping as many options on his table as possible. He had always lived in abundance, but suddenly, it seemed, he no longer cared about ensuring he had variety and plenty of options, he had become more focused on his future and ensuring that nothing could impact the freedom he was building for himself. He had come to realize over the last several days, that almost every woman in his life was a liability, a distraction from his ultimate goals of financial independence and freedom from the grind, not assets that could further his aims and goals. Fern, like none of the others was the greatest example of this, he thought, *what could she really add to his future, she brought literally nothing to the table that he could not buy for a mere few dollars if and when he wanted it*, or so he was beginning to convince himself. So then, why the hell did he let her get so close to everything? He couldn't answer that question. He had no awareness that the freedom he prized made him more like her than he realized.

There was another girl. Prettier. Younger. Looked just enough like Yuyi to make his stomach tense. He met her while shooting pool in one of the beer bars he had found while out riding. She was teasing. Aloof. A master of the pretend-disinterest trick.

But Chase had studied that trick, and had by now mastered it.

He flipped it on her when she asked him if he had WhatsApp. He had begun to make her chase. When she finally asked if he wanted to bar fine her and take her home, he didn't act like it really mattered one way or the other. He let her initiate everything. Slow, Needy. He knew she was desperate for a customer, with fifteen other girls working in that bar, many younger than her, nights went by with few even buying her a couple of lady-drinks. He knew he was the prize, that she needed his money, he didn't need to choose her, he was the one with options, not her. When she would message him every day, sometimes double and triple texting, he would wait to respond or not respond at all. He knew the rule was to never give out one's number to these girls, but he rarely followed it. If one became obtrusive, he could just block her. No big deal.

Then one evening when he had returned to shoot some more pool, and she had told him that she needed money because she was going back to Bangkok to live, he indicated that he could help her. It was then that she whispered, "You make me feel something I never feel before."

He smiled but didn't answer, "sure he thought, I'm special" and tried not to laugh out loud at the absurdity of the move, that by now he had seen too many times to ignore. Instead, he said "don't touch me" as she leaned against him, half joking, half serious, she couldn't, tell which. Soon she was practically begging him to take her. He agreed and the next morning, she didn't want to leave, offering him to let her stay with him until he went back to Patong, for the ridiculously low-rate of 1000 Baht a day. He declined and drove her back to her bar, and dropped her off, not buying her breakfast or even giving her a hug good bye before riding off and not looking back. He didn't want to think he was becoming jaded, just more realistic, and understanding that being nice to any woman, especially these girls, was a fool's errand, and undermined the respect that they may hold for him. He knew he didn't need to be a jerk, but being kind, wasn't in his favor, and the less so the better for him, especially.

FERN (internal, May 14th – Her Birthday)

She watched the time all day. Checked her messages obsessively. Every time her phone buzzed, her heart surged, only to sink again. He didn't write. Not even a "Happy Birthday." Had asked for the date twice, during the six months they had texted and had been excited to tell her about the surprises he had in store for her on their upcoming trip together, so she was holding out that he would try to make contact on that day. She found herself wondering what the surprise he had planned for her would have been. Based on how excited he seemed when he told her about it, she thought it might have been a big deal. But the day was slipping by, and nothing.

She stared at the screen like it owed her something. And then came the twist she didn't expect: She respected him more for it. He wasn't chasing. He wasn't begging. He was winning. And that made her nervous. Because if he could walk away from this... he could walk away from anything, and it could mean that she had read him incorrectly and that he was not as mentally weak as she had banked on him being. She rationalized, most wait the standard *30 Days* typical of the *No*

Contact Response, but something about the feel of silence screamed permanence that she found unsettling, she sensed his energy changing, and it wasn't what she had planned on.   Something else had begun to change as well, the sense of relief she had initially felt had dissipated.

FERN (internal)

He's coming back to Patong tomorrow. Eight more days in Phuket. If I let them pass... it's over.

She walked past the hotel where she knew he'd be staying. Paused. Looked inside.

Thought about leaving a note with the staff. Something cryptic but unmistakable. She thought that a real message, something he could hold in his hands would mean more than a WhatsApp message, that in part she was afraid to send out of simple fear of how she would feel if he had blocked her.

"We need to finish the story. – F"

But she hesitated. What if he ignored that too?

She walked on, telling herself that he would crack and make the next move first. Hoping that she was right.

CHASE (internal, May 15th)

He didn't feel broken anymore. Just refined.

He looked in the mirror: leaner. Eyes clearer. Sleep deeper, less troubled, dreams less chaotic and disturbing. Tomorrow, he would check into the Patong hotel for his final stretch.

He had no expectations. No agenda. Only intention. If Fern reappeared, fine. He would cross that bridge if and when he got to it.

If she didn't?

He'd already gotten the better deal - knowing that truth and that he had dodged a bullet.

Chapter Sixteen

The Past, the Present, the Pain

FERN (FLASHBACK – Khon Kaen, Age 9)

THE FLOOR OF THEIR house in Khon Kaen, during the summer of 1992 was always cool underfoot, the smooth concrete a relief from the humid weight of the air outside. Fern sat on the step just inside the doorway, knees pulled to her chest, arms wrapped around them like a shield. Outside, the dogs barked and a motorbike whined in the distance, fading into the rural hush of Isaan farmland. Inside, her mother was crying again—quiet this time, restrained. The kind of crying Fern had come to recognize as the worst kind. The kind that didn't stop.

Her father was in the other room, drunk again. The whiskey bottles never clinked loudly; he was careful like that. He was a ghost when he drank—pacing, muttering, sometimes kicking a wall, or a chair. When he didn't drink, he was quiet and distant, rarely speaking unless it was to issue a correction or deliver a complaint. He hadn't touched Fern in weeks. Not even to ruffle her hair.

That night, something changed.

She had been asleep in her room when the door opened. Not loudly, but with that slow, deliberate quietness that belied something ominous, something sinister. She smelled the alcohol first. Then heard the uneven breath. Her eyes stayed closed.

He sat on the edge of the bed, not touching her at first—just breathing. Then the blanket shifted, and his fingers traced the edge of her arm. Not a slap. Not a correction. Something else. Something that made her stomach knot and her throat close.

She didn't cry. She didn't move.

Eventually, he left, the door closing as softly as it had opened. But something had been taken from her that night—not in flesh, but in safety, in innocence, in defiance of the unspoken covenant between child and parent that said, you will protect me.

Her mother didn't ask why Fern stopped hugging her, didn't seem to even notice. Why she never asked for bedtime stories again. Why she started brushing her own hair and locking her door when she could, and why she spent so much more time alone in her room. Maybe she didn't want to know.

That was the week Fern started putting away her toys when no one asked, started smiling when she didn't feel like it, started hiding in plain sight. She understood, instinctively, that her needs were perceived as inconvenient, and that awareness hurt her deeply. That love was conditional. That being too much—even just emotional-ly—could push people away.

And that's when the first layer of the mask went on.

The persona of sweetness, of being the good girl. The mask of not needing. The Puella mask—the eternal girl, always light, always fun, always easy to be around. The one who never asks for more, never challenges, never expects to be chosen.

This was the birth of her avoidance of attachment, her choosing in-dependence over closeness.

From that foundation, Fern learned to seduce rather than connect. To enchant rather than expose. She became what people wanted to see. A chameleon. A fantasy. She learned to give affection without vulnerability, and receive attention without ever truly letting anyone in. She learned that control was safer than vulnerability and just as importantly, that she had something men wanted.

And when she grew older—when the lights dimmed and the music started and the club filled with men from other countries who wanted a piece of something exotic and soft—she knew exactly how to become what they needed.

Because she had practiced since she was nine years old, and believed that her strength came from mastering that persona and fulfilling that role regardless of the personal cost.

May 15th, 2025 – 4:14 AM – Patong.

The fan creaked above them, stirring the warm air without relief. The room was the size of a storage unit, its fluorescent bulb flickering faintly above a sagging mattress, makeup bags, laundry baskets, and a floor strewn with tangled clothes. On one wall, the flaking wallpaper barely held onto a yellowing poster of a K-pop idol. On the other, a photo of Fern and some friends from five years ago—before the drinks, the fatigue, and the slow erosion of something she never even had the words to name.

Fern sat on the edge of the mattress, legs curled beneath her, a beer in hand. Her makeup was still on—just smeared enough to suggest she hadn't washed her face since coming home. Two bottles lay empty on the floor. The third she was now halfway through.

She'd stopped trying to hide it from Fon. Fon, for her part, was smoking while texting a sponsor how much she missed him, and asking with only halfhearted interest when he was coming back to see her, one leg propped on the ledge, her hair wrapped in a towel, scrolling a second phone Fern wasn't supposed to know about.

Fern had just turned 33. And the only thing she felt was used up and alone.

FERN (internal)

What do I have to show for it? Ten years of dancing. Of fake smiles. Of watching girls half my age getting all the attention, all the tips. And now Chase... gone. Not a message. Not a meme. Not even a birthday wish.

She hated that it hurt. And hated even more that she still hoped he might reach out. She had built something with him—something more careful than with any other customer. She had curated texts. Planned moods. Shifted her language, her photos, her tone. She had invested herself. And for what?

She wanted to believe he cared. But maybe that was the biggest lie she'd ever sold—to herself.

Fon exhaled smoke into the muggy air. She turned and looked at Fern—disheveled, detached, slipping. "You gotta stop this," she said, voice flat. "He's gone. Men like that—they don't come back. Not for girls like us." Fern didn't reply. Fon stepped closer. Sat on the opposite edge of the mattress and produced a small pink pill. Held it between two fingers. "You need to stop feeling like shit. One of these. Just to clear your head."

Fern stared. "Yaba?" Fon nodded. "Not much. Just enough. Takes the edge off. Makes you forget the sadness. You think too much, Fern. You always did." Fern didn't take it. Not yet. But she didn't say no either. Fon smiled inside.

FON (internal)

She's almost done. Frayed. Soft. Easier to shape when they're like this.

The manager had stopped asking about Fern. But others in the syndicate still checked in. Chase had money, potential. They'd wanted her to keep him warm. Now, Fon saw her chance. She had already messaged one of their other operators. Just one line: "If he resurfaces, I'll take the lead."

She'd always resented how much space Fern took up. The fake sweetness, the childlike charm, the way she kept her bikini top on when the others danced topless. The crocodile tears. Now? Now she'd be the one they trusted.

Later that night, while Fern dozed on the mattress, head resting on a rolled-up shirt, Fon stepped out into the hall. She lit another cigarette and messaged a handler: "She's not responding well. Drinking more. Considering Yaba. He never wrote. Might try again when he checks in tomorrow." Then she returned, watched Fern sleep, and smirked. Inside, Fern stirred. She wasn't asleep. She was thinking—and aching.

The next morning, Fern walked back to see Pom—needing to be near the only person she didn't think wanted anything from her and the only person whose advice she thought she could honestly trust. The old woman behind the cart, graying and sharp-eyed, looked up and smiled.

"Late today," she said.

Fern sat, quiet. Ordered her standard beef and noodles, and then picked at her food, more pushing it around the bowl contemplatively than diving in voraciously like usual.

"You're tired," the woman said. "It's not the dancing. It's your soul, child. You've given too much to people who don't give back."

Fern bit her lip.

"Men can be anchors or knives," the old woman added. "This one... Chase. He was the first one who didn't make you feel dirty, wasn't he?"

Fern nodded. A tear slipped down without permission.

Pom reached over. Touched her wrist. "You'll only lose him if you act like the girl they expect. Don't go down with the rest. You still have time to leave the fire before it burns everything."

Fern looked away. But she held onto the words. She was scared and for the first time since she started dancing, confused about where her life was heading. The security she had thought she was creating by being an island unto herself was starting to feel like a lonely destination where she was trapped.

That night, back in the apartment, Fern opened her Notes app. Typed out a message she thought about leaving at the hotel desk. Something physical, something he could hold, something more personal than a WhatsApp message.

"We weren't finished."

She stared at it. Deleted it. Typed again:

"I miss you, Kha."

Deleted that too. Then, she tried:

"The ending is up to you. – F"

She hovered over "Send to Printer."

Fon came in. "You good?" Fern locked the screen. "Yeah. Just tired."

Fon smirked. "Get some rest. Big week ahead." They were being sent to Koh Larn to escort a Korean businessman for the weekend. Easy money. But also, more fakeness and filth than Fern felt she could stomach.

And somewhere, out past the balcony, past the lights of Bangla and the echo of basslines, a man was packing his bag for Patong.

CHASE (FLASHBACK – Northwestern Pennsylvania, Age 7)

January 7, 1979. It was dark and cold, negative four degrees Fahrenheit. The stars overhead were razor-sharp, and the moonlight etched a silver line across the snow-covered meadow in front of them. Seven-year-old Chase stood beside his father, both of them bundled in camouflage jackets and wool gloves, the cold biting through anyway. He didn't know the time, only that it was late. Late enough to feel like something secret was happening.

He would come to understand, years later, that this was no ordinary night. It was a rite. A lesson. Just the first in what would come in a long line of similar types of conditioning exercises. And it was a brutal one.

"Do you know why we're here?" his father asked, voice low.

"To kill a fox," Chase replied.

His father nodded. "And how are we going to do that, son?"

Chase hesitated. "I don't know."

His father smiled—thin, proud, cruel. "We're going to make it come to us. Make it believe it has a chance to get what it wants. What it needs to survive. And then we're going to take it, because we want something too. That's life, Chase. Get it before it gets you."

The green box at their feet whirred to life, and a distorted sound emerged: the screech of a rabbit in distress. High-pitched. Piercing. Raw. A recording of an animal in agony, likely injured and terrified as someone held a microphone to its mouth.

Chase felt the cry burrow into his chest like a hot needle. But he didn't move. Didn't show it.

His father scanned the white field with a red-lensed spotlight strapped to his hat. Fox couldn't see red—he had explained that earlier. Most animals are color blind and their eyes reflect back when hit with lights at night. The light wouldn't betray them, but it would catch in the predator's eyes like a shard of glass in the dark.

They waited. The tape looped. The rabbit kept screaming.

Then the hand came down on Chase's shoulder—steady, firm. "There," his father whispered.

The rifle cracked. A small shape crumpled in the snow.

Chase didn't speak. He didn't cry. But something inside him broke—not in fear, not in sadness, but in certainty. In the way a child sees the world before it's stained. He was part of it now. The deception. The bait. The taking. He had been made complicit in something irreversibly adult, and real.

And deep in that cold Pennsylvania field, he learned something he would never forget:

People came when they thought they'd get what they needed. And if you could control that belief—you controlled everything.

That night, Chase understood the currency of pain. Of illusion. Of emotional precision. And he never looked at life the same way again.

Chapter Seventeen

The Encounter

May 15th – Late Afternoon – Bangla Road

THE LATE AFTERNOON RAIN drizzled down between the thumping neon and gaudy signs of Bangla Road. The heat was thick, but Chase hardly noticed. His focus was on staying loose, staying in motion. The girl beside him clung to his arm with practiced affection. Her name was Gam—early thirties, pretty in a soft, delicate and unworn way, though last night she'd gotten embarrassingly drunk while they were out and made a minor scene at the late-night BBQ restaurant she had practically insisted, they go to.

"Can I stay again tonight?" she'd asked that morning, voice cracking slightly, trying to sound casual. Then she added I want to stay with you, here, watch movies together, eat together, sleep together."

He hadn't answered her. He hadn't needed to. He didn't say anything, just gave her an extended gaze and said he was going to eat lunch and do some shopping. The hesitation was enough. Still, she walked beside him now, matching umbrellas in hand, borrowed from the resort. She was feeding them both watermelon from wooden sticks out of a plastic bag, just purchased from a street vendor on Bangla Road. They were heading back to the room from lunch and a trip to the mall.

They passed Soi Sea Dragon like he had countless times before. But this time it wasn't just another entrance to another bar street.

She came from the right, her back to him, causing him to take a closer look, size was right, hair from behind was right, but it wasn't until she turned in profile that he knew for sure it was her.

Fern.

No makeup. No flash. A simple floral dress hung from her shoulders to just above the knee, not unlike the dress she wore when she met him at the airport except darker in color. Her phone and small hand purse in one hand, a small piece of something in the other. She stepped out from behind them, crossing their path—ostensibly to drop something in a trash bin in front of a street stall—but it was too precise, too quick, too directly into his path.

As she turned back towards the way she had come, their eyes locked.

Three seconds. Maybe four.

The look on her face was like that of a small animal, a rabbit, a kitten, something helpless, staring into the headlights of an oncoming truck. Not panicked—resigned, betrayed, sad and lost but hoping. Her eyes appeared pleading, but she too never broke stride just walked fast and low, like a cat who appears afraid of an approaching stranger. Had she studied the look to replicate it at this moment, it all appeared too staged, to calculated to ensure they saw one another, so she could read the look on his face and he the one on hers. Chase wasn't sure, and tried to calibrate how to handle the situation as it unfolded in front of him as if almost in slow motion.

Her eyes didn't widen or narrow. They pleaded, and they held. Stared into his.

His were masked behind a new pair of Aviators he had purchased a few days prior.

He didn't slow. Didn't speak. Didn't gesture, not so much as a nod in her direction. He just held her gaze for as long as she held his, but he kept walking, never breaking stride, never flinching. She was sure he had seen her, he had to have, but she wasn't completely sure he had, and later she would wonder, doubt only added to that which already existed.

It took everything in him not to say her name. To stop. To reach. But he didn't. Because he knew that wasn't his move to make. He had wanted to call out her name, almost did, but war wasn't always noise. He knew that sometimes, the silence was the sword. And today, he'd drawn blood by not unsheathing it.

He remembered something he had once read when studying Sun Tzu and traditional Chinese proverbs: *"If you wait by the river long enough, the bodies of your enemies will float by."* He wasn't angry with her, disappointed, yes, but he knew by now that life was not about experiencing disappointment and hurt, they were natural parts of it, and what mattered was how one responded when they surfaced. No, he was not angry, he was patient.

FERN (internal)

I saw him. With *her*. He looked... stronger. Leaner. Like the weight I thought he'd carry was never there at all. Like he'd dropped me like an old coat and moved on. *She* was taller, prettier, and had bigger boobs than I do. He hadn't collapsed; he had upgraded.

CHASE (internal)

I wanted to speak. But I couldn't. She threw the match. Let her live in the fire.

Later that Evening – Patong Beach

Chase watched the tide roll in, waves murmuring against the seawall. He was leaner now. The gym sessions, the long walks, the clean diet—they were paying off.

The collagen under his eyes had erased the shadows of stress. The Botox smoothed the lines of concern he carried in his daily life. He looked in the mirror each morning and saw a man ten years younger, but carrying twenty years more wisdom.

He missed Fern.

Not just her smile or her scent or the way she said "okay Na" when trying to sound cute.

He missed the version of his life that he had allowed himself to picture with her in three years, the plan they had begun to slowly formulate together, a dream—before she turned away.

But he loved his plan more. The dream of living in Thailand as his base of operations, with regular trips to other countries, slow travel, quietly, purposefully. Three years. Passive income growing steadily by the week. A life designed, not drifted into, or aimlessly passed through. His purpose had been set before he met her, before he considered pulling her into his flow, allowing her to share in his journey, affording her an opportunity to have something, build something, share something wonderful, exciting, special, and uniquely theirs. An epic adventure rooted in love, something timeless. It sold itself. He didn't need to force it on anyone, and if she wasn't interested, it was her loss, not his.

He would not deviate now.

That night, Gam lay curled on the bed beside him in his Patong Hotel, wrapped in one of his shirts, content and tired, scrolling on her phone. A romantic film played quietly on the screen—Memoirs of a Geisha. It had been his pick, one of his favorites, and he wanted to feel the sadness the film had always engendered in him. He watched, half-focused, half-haunted. The elegance, the sacrifice, the emotional seduction masquerading as grace, and the patience and discipline the characters were forced to master in order to survive. How love had evolved over a lifetime of sacrifice, secrets, and shadows.

Gam paused the film. Turned toward him.

"She like the girl in this movie," she said. "Not same job, but same sad heart. Same hope."

Chase smiled faintly, eyes wet, but not leaving the screen. "Yeah," he said. "She learns too late that not every man wants to own her. Some just want to understand her. But by then, she's learned to hide too well."

Gam tilted her head. "You mean Fern?"

Chase turned to her. "I mean all of them." He paused. "And me, too."

Gam gave a startled laugh as she reached over and touched his hand, "you cry" she said softly, surprised, her eyes studying him with confused interest. He didn't deny it. He just stared at the screen as the credits rolled and said "Allowing myself to feel something deeply makes me stronger and feel more alive." Gam blinked. "So...why this movie?"

His response left her speechless "Because," he said, voice steady, "there's something about watching someone survive with dignity in a world that's designed to break them but can't. And when you understand what that costs, and what they are willing to do for the one they love, ... the tears come for them and the beauty of their sacrifice, not for yourself."

That Night – Fern's Apartment

Fern sat on the edge of the mattress, still dressed, still clutching her phone. Her WhatsApp profile picture had been blanked for two days. A test. An appeal. A withdrawal?

Nothing.

She'd typed three messages and deleted them all.

"I saw you today." "You looked good." "I miss you."

Nothing felt true enough. Nothing felt safe.

Fon stepped into the room, fresh from the shower, towel-wrapped.

"You, okay?" she asked, not kindly, but with intent.

Fern didn't answer.

"You saw him, didn't you?" Fon lit a cigarette. "Did he see you?"

Fern nodded. "He didn't stop." She didn't elaborate that he was with someone else and that somehow within the few short weeks since she had ended it with him, he looked better, improved, and not the same man that had walked away in the garden that day. She was still processing those observations and her disbelief about them herself and knew that Fon didn't need any additional information that she could rub in her face.

Fon exhaled, a smirk curling at the edge of her mouth. "Good. Now you know. He's moved on." "You should be glad. Now you're free. Clean break." She saw that she was having the desired effect so she continued, "If he really loved you, he would have gone out of his way to convince you to stay, he would have been trying to win you back, but he hasn't done anything. What does that tell you? You were always just another whore to him." She hissed, with a smug sense of self-assuredness.

Fern flinched.

And she didn't feel confident. Initially, she had felt sadness but a strange sense of relief, like a pressure had been removed from her mind, and it had felt freeing, like she could stop hiding and worrying that she would be exposed somehow. But that initial release was being replaced with something much more haunting. She was no longer being seen. She felt cracked, and empty, and what's more it felt self-inflicted, not as if it had been done to her, it was the awareness that she did it to herself, let fear decide her fate, not daring.

Not the person he saw her as being, intrepid, his *Intrepid Little Renegade*, but for who she was always trying to hide, a scared little girl from Issan. Not who she wanted to be. Not the daring spy who completed missions with a fearlessness and grace, not the determined woman she wanted desperately to convey. Not the frame she carried while dancing.

She felt sad, lost and confused, and stuck in the same self-defeating patterns of life she could not seem to escape despite her best laid plans, intentions, and all the illusions she created for those around her, and what she was coming to realize, the illusions she had carefully crafted for herself. She had always prided herself on being independent, strong, and self-sufficient, but suddenly, and as a result of her decision to discard Chase, she felt a loneliness she hadn't felt in a long time. A loneliness she thought she could leave behind by staying perpetually detached.

The Next Morning – Noodle Cart

Pom's noodle stand smelled of broth and garlic and patience.

Fern sat silently as Pom stirred. "I saw him yesterday," Fern said at last.

Pom didn't look up. "With someone?"

Fern nodded.

"He see you?"

"Yes, I'm almost certain, he had to, I was right in front of him. He looked right at me. Didn't stop, just... walked."

Pom ladled soup into a bowl. "That's what men do when they've been hurt. The good ones, anyway. They don't scream. They don't beg. They leave. And they don't come back the same."

Fern's voice was barely above a whisper. "I thought he'd at least say something."

"And what would that have been, and what would you have said in return?"

Fern had no answer.

Pom sat beside her. "Do you remember what I told you? 'Distance proves a horse, time proves a man.' Well, time just gave you your answer."

Then Pom added, "you didn't see your plan through to the end. You didn't think through to what you would feel and do if he didn't speak to you, didn't beg for you, didn't wilt in front of you, and now you are more uncertain." Finally, she added, "you insist on playing a game with this man, rather than considering honesty, and now you don't know if he wants to keep playing it at all."

Fern stared down at the soup. Unmoving.

Pom continued. "A man who's comfortable by himself, that man is powerful. Not in the way that harms, but in the way that doesn't need. You didn't really see him as strong before, Fern. You mistook his acceptance of you, his caring, the attention he gave you freely as a sign of weakness, as evidence that something was broken in him.

And maybe at some point, something had been broken, but he had fixed it, and he was open to loving you, willing to risk, to be hurt again, because of who he thought you may be, and because perhaps he does not fear that which had never destroyed him before. heart-ache. And now you can't see yourself through his eyes anymore. And that's what's haunting you."

"He didn't want to own you," Pom said gently. "He wanted to see you become what you're capable of, and possibly even share a life together. That's rare. But it's scary too—because now that he's gone, you can't keep pretending to be okay with being less. And you've lost the only mirror that showed you who you could've been. So, you avoid, like always, because letting someone love you fully... that's the same as handing them the sword to cut you wide open."

"You think keeping a man like Chase at arm's length makes you strong," Pom had said, not unkindly. "But maybe it just means you never have to find out what you're worth when the games are gone. That's the real fear, isn't it? Not that he'll stop loving you. But that he won't... once he really sees you."

Fern swallowed. She bit her lip. "I don't know how to fix it."

Pom smiled gently. "Maybe you're not supposed to fix it. Maybe you're supposed to become the woman he saw in you. And if you do... maybe that'll be enough."

Chase continued wrestling with his own demons. The self-doubt that sinks in as a man gets older; his body struggling to make gains and maintain ground once held. Surviving in a world that competes for everything even if you don't want to be in the competition. Thinking, hoping, that for once he had found someone who he could let down the guard that had kept him sharp, disengaged, alone, for all these years, only to find that it was that closeness that he sought that she feared the most. And the worst part, that he should have known, likely did know, but chose to ignore, allowing the worst evil of all to take hold - hope.

He had come to listen for that word when trying to gauge what type of person he was dealing with. As a person that *planned*, he had seen the difference in the effectiveness with which people lived their lives. Those that planned, often did, those that hoped, often waited, passively, expecting that somehow the things they wanted in life, their dreams, ambitions, goals, all would somehow magically manifest if they could just visualize and wait.

He wasn't sure; he had put in effort, been consistent, honest, respect-ful, present. Yes, he hoped she would respond, but he took action, planned, instilled vision, validated her, tried to pull and hold her into his frame and yet, when the time came to move things to another level, one that would force them to be real, and not just words on a screen, she fled, retreated, dismissed, discarded.

It was classic Avoidant behavior, and consistent with the Puella Eterna dynamic he had now come to see so clearly in her. She was not inca-pable of love, she was terrified of the loss of control the feelings engen-dered, and she pushed away anything and anyone that threatened her sense of safety - at one point in time a survival mechanism, now likely a lonely fortress. One in which she can, in her mind, play the process of waiting for her Prince, only to drive him away when he approaches the outer walls. Fooling herself that the illusion of control she exerts over her professional life will somehow be enough when the neon lights finally fade once and for all. She had given him glimpses over the last six months of her avoidant style of attachment, but he either ignored or minimized the significance of what she was saying.

At last, he decided, you can't catch a terrified animal by running it down or chasing it. If you want it, you have to be patient, establish trust, it has to obtain a sense of safety in your orbit, or it will never get close enough to you and he knew it was that kind of patience he needed to be strong enough now to maintain. He needed to hold the space, and he understood that his worth wasn't contingent upon her courage to reciprocate love, it had been built through his hard work and focus on his purpose, and that was unwavering.

They had started a game, both complicit in its origins and develop-ment. A game rooted in seduction, the rules of attraction, not logic, but emotion, and now the primary emotions were fear, longing, and pride. She may have used the fear as a real excuse to create separation and uncertainty, banking on the fact that doing so would further his obsession, while returning to her a sense of control she feared she had lost. And now, perhaps his only chance left at winning, was if she had entangled herself in her own web and had become obsessed herself.

Chase reflected on a comment Fern had made once, when talking about why she thought the transactional nature of her work kept things safe for her when she said, "when they pay, you leave, it's nothing more, nothing personal, and there is then no opportunity for them to destroy you." It didn't register at the time, he wasn't able to fully comprehend what she was saying, but now in hindsight it was her revealing a truth about herself, emotional connection equated to vulnerability which was threatening to her sense of safety. She feared the love she longed for, and perhaps deep down inside, she didn't feel she deserved, or that anyone would be willing to truly give in a way that would ever feel safe.

Chapter Eighteen

The Day Before
the Storm

THE MORNING BROKE WITH a hush across Patong Beach, the sky a
dull gray gauze that pressed low and intimate, filtering the sun into
something cool and diffused. A light rain misted the air like memory—soft, reluctant, full of ghosts. Chase walked slowly along the me-
andering path that ran parallel to the beach. *"Survivors"* by Passenger
drifted through his AirPods, the aching words syncing with the hush
of the waves and the rhythmic patter of rain against his umbrella.

Surprisingly, his mood was light. Not euphoric—he was far too tem-
pered for that—but unburdened. Peaceful. He found himself smiling
at the Thais sweeping the sidewalk and unlocking their beach carts.
They all smiled back. There was no more expectation of contact, of
redemption, or reunion. He had accepted that Fern would not reach
out. The wound remained, yes, but it had stopped bleeding. He had
begun to feel, at least in moments, that he was unencumbered by her
drama and the chaos that her pullback had created.

His final workout at the gym near Soi Nanai was methodical and hard, but satisfying. He pushed himself past his limits, past the memories of her touch and voice and laughter, until the pain of exertion drowned the ache of memory. Afterward, he showered, dressed simply, and walked to the Balinese restaurant that had become a must visit spot on his trips to Phuket, the BBQ place he had always planned to take Fern. He ate alone—ribs, avocado salad, and soda water. The seat across from him stayed empty. He didn't mind. Being alone had always been a defining feature of his life and was something he had accepted years ago.

In the early afternoon, he settled into a beer bar off Second Road, a familiar place near the gym, just a few doors down from where he and Fern had ended their first night together. It had been there, over clinks of pool balls and the sting of her offering up another girl, that Chase first caught a glimpse of her mask slipping. Today, the rain tapped gently on the metal awning overhead, and the light was golden in the way only tropical rainstorms make it—ripe, saturated, cinematic.

He flirted lightly with a bar girl, a tall, elegant woman with sharp cheekbones and a tattoo of a dragon winding up her back. There was no spark, no danger, but there was warmth. Connection, even if shallow. He paid her bar fine without hesitation. He wasn't going to sleep alone on his last night.

The shower they took together was slow and hot. Not just sensual, but human. Her hands traced him without questions, and he welcomed the distraction of skin on skin. Their sex was intense but unburdened. She didn't ask about his thoughts, didn't pretend to be anything but what she was—a woman in his bed, for tonight only. Afterward, they dressed and walked to a local seafood spot where the tables spilled onto the sidewalk under strings of yellow bulbs.

Earlier while at the beer bar, he had watched her prepare a bowl of spicy soup, her hands expertly chopping lemongrass, bird chilies, and lime. She shared it with two other girls, the three of them dipping sticky rice into the broth with fingers, chatting and giggling in Thai. Now, with a Blue Hawaiian in front of her, she was taking selfies, smiling brightly as the seafood arrived: grilled prawns, oysters with chili, whole steamed fish, and clams in basil and broiled lobster. "I eat more now than all week," she joked.

Chase nodded, amused but detached. His mind was elsewhere. He was watching her, but not really seeing her. The ghost of Fern stood between them, silent and omnipresent.

Later, in bed, they watched a Thai series about revenge. A scene flickered on-screen: a girl photographing a man walking by on the street, sending it immediately to someone unseen. Chase sat up slightly. His mind drawn back to what he had witnessed two days prior while sitting in a roadside beer bar. One of the bar tenders had quickly taken a photo of a Farang walking down the other side of the street and then texted it to someone. She had zoomed in on the man's face prior to attaching the original and the cropped version to her message. He had observed the action and had made note in his mind, and now a flood of questions surfaced.

"Hey," he said softly. "Does that happen? Do bar girls take pictures of men and send them to other people?"

She smiled, too casually. "Sure. Everyone watches."

"Even if the guy never saw her?"

She laughed. "Even then. We have friends. We help each other."

Chase's heart tightened. "What if someone asked a friend to take a picture of a Farang and text them if he walked by? Would that be normal?"

She nodded, chewing her thumbnail. "Yes. It happens."

The realization rippled through him like static—Fern. The day he ran into her on Bangla, the chance encounter... wasn't chance. She'd known. She'd had him under surveillance. He was the mark, and she was the ghost pulling strings. Even when absent, she played the game. Then he remembered back to the day he had returned to Patong from Rawai. He had been walking back to his hotel after a few rounds of beers at a local bar when he thought he recognized a girl from a photo Fern had sent him one night after work at her favorite late-night BBQ. The new friend she had made at work. The woman had been walking slightly behind him on the opposite side of the road, and when he had turned and saw her, how she balked, and turned back quickly and walked in the other direction as if she had "been made". He dismissed the experience at the time as a combination of wishful thinking and paranoia, now he wasn't so sure. None of it mattered now anyway. He had come back to Phuket planning on spending the month with Fern, getting to know one another on a deeper level with the hope that something lasting could develop, and he had spent it trying to forget her. The trip was over, and while it wasn't a complete bust, he had to be honest with the sense of disappointment he felt inside over how everything had played out.

The next morning, heavy rain lashed the pavement as his cab wound through the waking streets of Patong. The city was quieter, soaked and reverent. On the way to the airport, a WhatsApp message blinked into his phone.

[Three Messages]

1. I like this song.

2. I want you to listen to it.

3. I want to be one of all your women. One of the girls.

It was from the bar girl in Rawai. The one he had bar fined twice, who had never asked for money to stay the night, who had spent long hours beside him watching films, listening more than speaking. The link opened a video: *"One of the Girls"* – The Weekend, Jennie, Lily-Rose Depp.

He paused, let the song wash over him. The longing in her message, the vulnerability—it was real. Not deep, maybe, but true in its way.

He typed:

You always will be, Khub.

And meant it in the moment even though he knew he would never see her again. She would go down as just another in a long line of memories that would fade with time, and he reflected on how people seemed to pass through his life, coming and going at times in such unpredictable ways. The only thing he felt he knew for sure was that if you wanted a woman to stick around, you had better not treat her too well, show her too much respect, or let her know too much about you or your vulnerabilities. That, he reminded himself was the surest way to ensure they left you, and often without warning.

As the cab approached the departure terminal, watching the lights smear across the rain-streaked window, Chase let the weight of everything settle in his chest like smoke.

What he and Fern had—whatever it had been—was too complicated to call real and too powerful to call false. It was both. Maybe that was the truth he'd have to come to accept: some connections live in the space between sincerity and illusion.

He remembered a line from The Mayor of Kingstown when Milo the Russian pimp was talking to Iris, the high-priced escort. *The con, when done right, feels like love.* And maybe love, when it's raw and desperate and half-hoped for, feels like the perfect con. *Because it doesn't get old. It doesn't wear out.* It just lingers in the blood, a phantom heartbeat, even when the body's moved on.

He hadn't been the only one acting. They both wore masks—and both had bled underneath them. As his departure time approached, Chase listened as the rain poured on the roof above the lounge listening to the quiet storm inside his mind.

He had come for mystery, romance, and danger. He'd gotten all three. But not all with Fern. And that was the paradox. He had found what he was looking for, but not in the place he had wanted it to be.

And yet, he had gotten what he needed: clarity and growth. The month he had just lived through had wizened him in ways he could not have anticipated prior to his arrival just a few short weeks ago. Her presence in his life had served a purpose, was still serving a purpose, and the fact that they had crossed paths cosmically was not random or by chance. They were intended to serve a role in each other's life. Perhaps she was meant to teach him something and perhaps he was an opportunity for her to not only learn, but change her life as well. While he couldn't say how he had impacted her life, if he did at all, he knew her role had served its purpose for he was not the same man who had boarded that plane at LAX four weeks ago.

Fern had disappeared for reasons that were not as simple as rejection, or greed, or manipulation. Maybe she had started with the con—maybe even with a plan to hook, extract, and discard. But somewhere along the way, something real had taken root. He had succeeded in breaking through her professional façade, he knew that, and ironically, knowing that now was small consolation for what he felt was a missed opportunity to have something deeper with someone who he saw profound value in as a person. While he knew to not judge a person on his perception of their potential, he couldn't help but hope she could tap into that sense he had of her and grow into it by shedding the impact her past experiences had on how she felt about herself deep down inside. But that was not for him to decide or wait for, but for her to realize and grow from, if she could.

He knew now she was avoidant. That her Puella Eterna complex—forever the girl, never the woman—had cornered her into emotional self-destruction. She feared closeness. She feared her own feelings. And when he got too close, when it began to feel too much like love, she did what avoidants do: she fled. Withdrawing to her illusions of control and detachment from true intimacy or the risk of anyone seeing who she saw herself as underneath it all.

People usually take their aptitudes, intelligence, and God given gifts for granted, and Fern was no different. She didn't see those things in herself until they were reflected back by Chase, and him seeing them forced her to reconcile her life's choices and decide to either accept them as all she could be or change and that was too threatening.

She let him go not because she didn't care, but because she did. And because she didn't know how to hold both love and fear in the same hand.

He respected that.

And he mourned it.

They were mirrors—both longing for connection but running from its consequences. Both drawn to freedom and solitude, but craving intimacy too deeply to admit. What they had wasn't false. It was fractured.

Fern had, perhaps, saved him from her. Perhaps that was her mercy.

Chase had changed.

He was stronger now. More focused. The time in the Forge had refined him, stripped away illusion. He no longer needed to chase women for meaning, and he would not accept breadcrumbs of affection or strategic silence. If Fern ever returned, it would have to be real. Not a seduction. Not a game. But a reckoning.

And she would have to come to him whole—or not at all.

Back in Patong, the rain continued. Fern sat by the window in her room above the bar, watching the tuk-tuks splash through puddles below.

Fon lit a cigarette beside her. "You, okay?"

Fern shrugged, eyes distant. "He didn't message."

"You thought he would?"

She didn't answer.

The ache in her chest was a dull pressure, like a bruise under skin. She had expected to feel triumphant. Free. But she just felt hollow. She thought of him on the plane, listening to their songs, maybe replaying their moments in his mind. She hoped he would. She feared he wouldn't.

She whispered to herself, too quietly for Fon to hear:

"Attraction isn't logic. It's emotion. You have to instill intense emotion. We had that. We still do." But emotion, like rain, eventually dries. She continued to question if she had made a mistake in hoping that a man like Chase could ever really love a woman who does what she does for a living and if a woman like her could ever let herself be loved. She was tired of pretending to not need anyone. The energy it took to keep that false belief in place was exhausting her and draining her light. The accumulating years of illusion, drink, random and faceless men, and having to thread the needle created by the cognitive dissonance required to maintain her professional frame was taking its toll. She needed to get out, to learn to be happy with a life that returned her dignity and to once and for all stop worshiping at the idol of money, or her mother's validation, and she questioned if she had the strength remaining to walk away. Not because she ever hoped to get him back, but because he had shown her that she deserves it.

The story wasn't over. But the chapter had closed.

Chase was flying home. Fern was watching the street. Both of them changed, and changing still. Mirrors turned away.

But somewhere in the space between them, a connection still pulsed. Fragile. Flickering. Waiting.

For what, neither could say. But they both knew the truth now:

The fire they played with had left its scar.

Later that evening, as the rain slowed to a mist and Patong glistened under wet neon, Fern slipped on a black hoodie and walked alone toward the edge of town. She passed shuttered shops and the occasional tuk-tuk splashing by, until the flickering glow of Pom's noodle stand came into view. A tarp flapped in the breeze. Steam rolled from the battered cart where broth simmered and the scent of garlic filled the air.

Pom looked up as she approached, a sly smile spreading across her weathered face. "Late night? Or early soul?"

Fern pulled back the hood. Her eyes were tired, but clear. "Both."

She gestured to the rickety stool across from her. "Sit. You want the usual?"

She nodded. "Extra chili."

Pom ladled noodles into a bowl, humming. Fern watched her in silence.

"He left already?" she asked without turning.

She didn't need to ask who. "Yes. This morning."

"And you didn't say goodbye?"

"He didn't reach out," she said softly. "And I didn't either."

Pom handed her the bowl and sat across from her, wiping her hands on a towel.

"So? That mean it's over?"

She didn't answer right away. Stirred her noodles. Took a bite.

Then: "He was different. Not just the way he looked at me—but the way he listened. Like I wasn't just... a Go-Go dancer and a whore."

Pom nodded. "Dangerous. Men like that—make you forget who you are. Or worse, remind you."

Fern smiled faintly. "I think I wanted him to save me. Then got scared when I realized he might try."

"Or that you might let him."

She nodded.

"But still you let him go."

"I couldn't hold him and hold myself together at the same time."

Pom leaned forward, voice low. "You know what I think? You let him go not just to protect yourself—but to protect him. You felt too much. That was the danger."

Fern looked at her, tears not far from her eyes. "He would've waited. He would've kept building if I'd asked, if I'd given him anything. He wasn't afraid like me."

"But you didn't."

"Because I wasn't ready to be someone worth staying for. I'm too scared and too greedy."

The rain had stopped. Silence spread between them like steam over soup.

"You'll see him again?" Pom asked.

"Maybe. If he'll still have me. But only if I'm different. Only if I can come back real."

Pom smiled, standing. "Then start becoming."

Fern looked down at her bowl. Then back up, eyes shining with something between pain and resolve.

"I think I already have."

Chase's phone buzzed as he approached the boarding gate. He didn't reach into his pocket right away, because he didn't want to know it wasn't her messaging him. He just knew it wasn't, but the thought that it might be was better than knowing the truth.

It was Yomiko with a simple "I miss you". He waited to respond, out of habit and indifference. Then with just a simple emoji of him holding her dog Lucky in his arms, nothing more, not a word back. Then he turned his phone off and boarded the plan, walking slowly, deliberately away from his future, Phuket.

He had an excruciatingly long seven-hour layover in Hong Kong, and as he deplaned and made his way through security towards the lounge, he turned his phone back on. Yomiko had messaged him back with an emoji of her holding Lucky, and nothing else. She's trying to mirror me he thought, match my energy, not appear needy any more than she is able. He didn't care, but was thoughtful of why he didn't.

In many ways she was perfect for him. The only woman besides Julz, who he could continue to have satisfying sex with and still want to come back, even if he didn't care about permanence. He didn't know why sustained intimacy, emotional connection long-term was hard for him, but it was. In that respect, he supposed he was like Fern, avoidant, until he found a mirror, and then at least for her, he became anxious to not lose *her*. Ironically, he thought, it was exactly that anxiety that caused him to behave in ways that resulted in what he feared would happen. Her leaving. He was tired of second guessing.

An hour later, the bar-girl from Rawai hearted his last message and an hour after that Waan, messaged him: "I miss you Chace, kiss emoji" then "are you well?" His response, delivered thirty minutes later: "I'm the same, how's your eye?" She had told him that she had gone to the clinic the day or two prior due to an eye infection. "I'm fully recovered" she replied.

"Great, I'm in Hong Kong."

Her: "Oh you're home".

Chase: "No, layover, fly to LA in four hours."

Waan: "Okay, see you next year. You can call me anytime. Miss you," followed by two sad crying face emojis.

Chase: "I'll be back in six months; you can message me too."

Waan: "Okay hug & kiss emojis". He didn't respond.

Then twenty minutes after that three messages, triple texts, from Ing: "travel safely. I have a fever, headache and cough. I woke up late so I didn't say goodbye to you on the morning of your departure." The day prior she had offered to meet him for dinner and to stay the night then drive him to the airport the next morning, but he declined. He thought of her as a friend, and wasn't interested in sharing his bed with her and didn't feel like having to navigate declining her offer for a night together but then accepting a ride the next day to the airport. He mused on why he wasn't interested in a Thai woman who had her shit together, a family business, houses in Phuket and Bangkok, and land she leased to local farmers, not a sex worker.

Both sets of messages made the past three weeks of silence from Fern sound like a rifle shot.

He reflected on Waan's messages, and how that was how it had started with Fern, he felt for a second like he might be going crazy and said to himself, I'm not going through this again. But the truth was, she wasn't her, and would never be. She was sweet, cute, gave herself freely, easily, wanting, but there wasn't the spark, not the emotional connection at least on his part, so he found himself asking why was he even bothering.

Just repeating old habits, patterns he was determined to change, he didn't want or need another woman in the rotation. Wasn't sure if, at least for now, he even wanted the rotation he already had. He had decided that as a man, he had to rule his life through reason, and could no longer let it be ruled by a simple desire for the momentary passions he could feel through relationships with women. In that moment, a shift occurred, *she* no longer had the pull on him *she* had before. He was letting go of the illusion of who he wanted *her* to be, seeing *her* for who and what *she* was.

Complex, a creature who adapted to survive in a world of illusion, perhaps not someone broken completely yet, but someone under the surface who was scared and truly alone in the world. In that way he held onto respect for *her*. And truly wished *her* only the best.

Perhaps he would just focus on his purpose. His work, his health and fitness, and with building wealth and solidifying and possibly speeding up his retirement dream. The illusions of intimacy in Thailand were draining. So many women, so willing to dance the dance with you, and let you take them as far as possible, all working angles, so that it was hard to ever know for sure if anything but the hustle was ever real.

He had pulled it off too, in a weird sense. He had broken through her professional frame and perhaps even only for a while had been inside her heart. He just could not have imagined the emotional price that game would take on him. While he didn't think he had won *the game*, he considered it a stalemate, and for him, that was the closest thing to a victory he could have ever really hoped for against a far superior opponent like *her*.

He returned home with a story, a romantic one for sure, but he wasn't refreshed, he was seasoned, and he wasn't sure if the exhaustion he felt was from the jet lag or the emotional drain from the games inherent in the illusions of love in paradise.

Epilogue – Chase's Internal Reflection

CHASE SAT ON HIS Yamaha Super Tenere, on Angeles Crest Highway overlooking the San Gabriel Valley, the heat from the engine matching his thoughts. He finally admitted to himself what he'd known for a long time but had refused to truly see: the obsession he'd felt for Fern wasn't love—at least, not entirely. It was a puzzle he'd tried desperately to solve that not only involved her, but himself as well. It wasn't that she was irreplaceable; it was that she was impossibly unavailable.

She gave me just enough to keep me starving, he thought, a half-smile of bitter realization tugging at his lips. Just enough closeness to feel chosen, and just enough distance to never feel safe. Exactly what I'd trained my whole life to want.

He thought back to the countless women who had come and gone in his life, none sticking, each dismissed with practiced detachment. Fern had become the mirror of his own hidden fears and his deepest desires—the craving for intimacy without risk, the fantasy of being known without exposure. She was the emotional equivalent of an addictive substance, her intermittent reinforcement perfectly calculated, yet instinctive, ensuring he would always reach but never fully grasp. The emotional gauntlet she would lay for him to walk through with the vague references to her customers or her sexual fantasies, all strategically paired with regular messages to create an emotional roller coaster that kept him hooked.

And now, so many months later, Chase knew it had to stop. The puzzle that was *her* wasn't his to solve. He couldn't heal *her* wounds any more than she could heal his. She had been both muse and torment, teaching him not how to love, but how to identify exactly why he couldn't. Understanding this meant letting go not only of *her* but of the twisted comfort their toxic dance had provided.

She was never mine to keep, he reminded himself quietly, and I was never hers, as he continued his ride homeward. The road hummed under his tires as he leaned the machine into one turn after another. He felt the lessening of his obsession, leaving behind it something clean, strong, and more confident.

Dusk was settling over the valley as Chase raced towards his home and his future. The day had been wonderful, a nice score at the track, the wad of bills pressing against his leg as he rode, the puzzle of the All Turf Pick Three at least solved for that day, along with the one of Fern that had vexed him for the past six months since his return from Phuket. He hadn't thought about her constantly over the last several weeks, like before, and as the song changed to Savatage's *Edge of Thorns*, he found his mind momentarily drawn back to the image of her under the neon lights of the club, the first time their eyes met.

As he tucked into another hairpin turn, the opening lines of the song filled his ears, just as the car in the oncoming lane rounded the bend into view, taking up more than half his lane. Chase didn't have to time to react. The last image that flashed through his mind was of Fern looking over her shoulder, their eyes meeting, and her smile. The last words Chase uttered under his breath just before impact: *"Fuck it"* then the world went black, the chorus to the song continuing to play through his earbuds into the darkness.

Epilogue – Fern's Conversation with Pom

Fern sat across from Pom at the noodle stand, late enough that the street around them had gone quiet, the lights dimmed to muted amber hues. Pom looked up, patient and wise as always, her eyes softening when she saw the distress hidden behind Fern's carefully composed expression.

"You look like a woman who finally understands something she wishes she didn't," Pom observed gently, ladling broth into a steaming bowl.

Fern sighed, fiddling absently with a chopstick. "I keep asking myself why I couldn't stop thinking about him. Chase was just another man. Just another customer."

Pom smiled knowingly. "We both know that's not true."

Fern hesitated, her voice dropping to a near whisper. "He was safe, Pom. Not because he wasn't dangerous—he was dangerous—but because I never truly had him. And because I never had him, I felt I couldn't lose him." She paused, swallowing hard. "But now... he's really gone."

Pom reached out, placing a gentle, reassuring hand over Fern's. "You only thought he was safe because he wasn't like you—avoidant, afraid, unwilling to fully let himself feel. You saw yourself in him, and that frightened you, Fern. You ran from intimacy because deep down you didn't believe you deserved it."

Fern felt the sting of truth tightening her throat, the years of defenses slipping painfully. "But now I see him everywhere. In the empty chairs, in the faces of strangers. And it hurts, Pom, because I finally see what he really was." Pom tilted her head, her expression compassionate but firm. "And what's that?"

Fern looked away, eyes glistening with tears she refused to let fall. "The only man who ever wanted to love the real me—the one behind the mask, the one underneath the illusion. And I threw him away because that meant being truly seen, truly vulnerable."

Pom squeezed her hand gently. "Now you know what it cost you. Use that pain, child. Let it teach you how to stop running from love."

Fern looked up at the rain, washing away the city's grime, just as Chase's consistent presence had once been a promise to her that would wash away her past. For the first time in years, she didn't fear vulnerability—she mourned its loss. The realization felt heavy but strangely liberating, a first step toward a new way of living.

The next morning, she walked in, rather than past the door to the daily meeting of the local chapter of Alcoholics Anonymous. She had walked past the meeting location at least a dozen times before without ever entering. The feeling she had was reminiscent of the first time she stepped on stage. She wasn't sure she was ready yet to share, but she was willing to listen and to change.

Epilogue - Patong Beach, Phuket – Three Months Later

Fern sat alone in the quiet stretch of sand at the northern end of Patong Beach, far enough from Bangla's neon glow to feel separated from the chaos, yet close enough to remind her how easily she'd once slipped into its comforting anonymity. She held her phone loosely, her thumb tracing circles over the screen that had recently shattered her carefully constructed peace.

It had come in the form of a simple Facebook post, shared by a young woman whose profile picture Fern instantly recognized—a young woman with Chase's eyes. The message was brief but poignant:

"My dad, Chase, had a serious motorcycle accident this weekend. Doctors aren't sure when or if he'll pull through. Please keep him in your thoughts and prayers."

Fern's breath paused sharply, her heart seizing with an intensity she hadn't known herself capable of feeling. It had been months since she had seen Chase, months since she had ended things, convincing herself she had done so for both of their sake. Yet this news had cracked open every hidden corner of her heart, forcing her to confront something she'd tried desperately to bury.

She stood slowly, letting the damp sand cling between her toes as she stepped closer to the gentle surf, the rhythm of waves a quiet pulse beneath her own racing heartbeat. Her thoughts drifted back to that last conversation with Pom, words she'd replayed nightly since then, words she had come to understand held the key to her healing.

"You ran from intimacy," Pom had told her, firm yet compassionate, *"because deep down you didn't believe you deserved it."*

She knew Pom was right. Every step she'd ever taken had been away from true connection, hiding herself behind masks of charm, seduction, transactional affection. Chase had threatened those defenses simply by seeing her—not the version she presented to customers, not the calculated illusion, but her authentic self, broken and vulnerable. His gaze had burned through her carefully built defenses, leaving her raw and terrified, prompting her retreat.

Fern lifted her phone again, pulled toward a familiar message thread she'd never fully deleted. She hesitated, thumb hovering over the screen, the soft glow illuminating her conflicted expression. She'd already known Chase was writing their story—yet seeing the published book for sale, the cover pulsing with neon green letters, had stunned her, made her feel strangely important yet impossibly small.

She had read it twice in the last two days, each page a mirror reflecting truths she'd spent her life avoiding and memories she'd never forget. He had captured her essence, her illusions, and her truths, each chapter a quiet revelation that left her stripped bare. The final page haunted her most—a simple dedication that broke and healed her simultaneously:

"For F, who taught me love through letting go, and truth through illusion."

It wasn't anger or embarrassment she felt—it was grief. Grief at the loss of something genuine she'd dismissed out of fear, grief at her inability to accept love when offered honestly. Chase had seen her clearly, without judgment, without expectation. He had been able to love despite fear, and walk away with dignity when it wasn't reciprocated, a strength so rare she couldn't fathom it. And that knowledge had shaken her to her core, dismantling barriers she'd thought impenetrable.

She crouched low, fingertips brushing gently across the cool surf. With her other hand, she retrieved the delicate Wadee flower tucked behind her ear, symbolic of renewal and hope. Holding it close, she whispered softly, her voice barely audible over the waves:

"I'm sorry, Chase."

She laid the flower gently onto the water, watching as the waves carried it gently away. It drifted further, disappearing into the darkness, as if bearing her apology toward a man lying somewhere between life and death, dreams and reality.

Fern stood, the night breeze cooling the tears slipping down her cheeks. She took a deep, steadying breath. Tomorrow would bring another AA meeting—another careful step toward the vulnerability she'd spent her life fleeing. She was ready now. Not because the fear was gone, but because she understood that true strength came not from hiding behind illusions but in daring to face what lay beneath them.

She turned slowly from the sea, her path now clearer than ever. Whether Chase woke from his coma or remained suspended in that uncertain space, he had already changed her life irrevocably. He had shown her who she was capable of becoming—a woman who could be brave enough to confront her fears, a woman worthy of love.

As she walked toward the road, a gentle rain began falling, washing softly across her face, cleansing and calm, like the healing Chase had quietly promised from the very beginning.

Fern smiled gently into the night; her whisper carried softly on the breeze.

"I hope you wake up. And if you do, I hope you'll still remember me."

With quiet resolve, she moved forward, leaving behind illusions, stepping finally and purposefully toward truth, and hopefully one day, love.

·

·

·

·

·

·

·

·

·

·

·

·

•

•

•

•

•

•

•

•

•

•

•

Sources & Selected Works Referenced and Cited in This Novel

Literature & Fictional Influences

- Leather, Stephen. Private Dancer. (2005)

- Hallinan, Timothy. Queen of Patong. (2009)

- Hallinan, Timothy. The Jasmine Bar. (2008)

- Puzo, Mario. Fools Die. (1978)

- Hesse, Hermann. Demian. (1919)

- Puzo, Mario. The Godfather. (1969)

- The Blether. Thailand: The Vicious Truth About Thai Hookers. 9 Sep. 2015, Kemah Bay Marketing. Audiobook edition.

Psychology & Attachment Theory

- Bowlby, John. Attachment and Loss: Volume 1 – Attachment. (1969)

- Levine, Amir & Heller, Rachel. Attached: The New Science of Adult Attachment and How It Can Help You Find—and Keep—Love. (2010)

- Johnson, Sue. Hold Me Tight: Seven Conversations for a Lifetime of Love. (2008)

- CCC Psychological Services, Inc. Consulting Services.

Philosophy, Strategy, and Power Dynamics

- Tzu, Sun. The Art of War. Translations vary; widely cited for its aphorisms on deception and strategy.

- Greene, Robert. The 48 Laws of Power. (1998)

- Greene, Robert. The Art of Seduction. (2001)

Music & Cultural References

- Pat Benatar, *Love Is a Battlefield*. Chrysalis Records, 1983.

- Savatage, *Edge of Thorns*. Atlantic Records, 1993.

- Mötley Crüe, Starry Eyes. 1981 BMG Rights Management (US) LLC.

- Passenger, *Survivors* 2018 Black Crow Records under exclusive license to Nettwerk Music Group Inc.

- Camila Cabello, *Consequences, Never Be the Same.* Epic Records, 2017.

- Tuk Smith & The Restless Hearts, *Little Renegade.* Gypsy Rose Records, 2024.

Film & Television

- Memoirs of a Geisha. Dir. Rob Marshall, 2005.

- The Mayor of Kingstown. Created by Taylor Sheridan and Hugh Dillon, Paramount+, Season 2, Episode 8.

- The Notebook. Dir. Nick Cassavetes, 2004.

- *Revenge.* Directed and written by Coralie Fargeat, performances by Matilda Lutz, Kevin Janssens, Vincent Colombe, and Guillaume Bouchède, Charades, MES Productions, Monkey Pack Films, Logical Pictures, Nexus Factory, Umedia, uFund, Canal +, Cinémage 12, 2017Mr. McMahon. Directed by Andrew J. Muscato. Netflix, 2024.

Cultural Context & Setting

- Firsthand accounts and cultural commentary on Patong nightlife and the sex tourism economy of Phuket, Thailand.

- Informal street interviews and observational research in Patong, Rawai, and Khon Kaen.

www.ingramcontent.com/pod-product-compliance
Lightning Source LLC
Chambersburg PA
CBHW060137130626
46556CB00006B/2378

* 9 7 9 8 9 9 3 0 4 0 0 1 1 *